## "If you touch me I will scream,"

Marie muttered in impotent rage. "And when my disappearance is discovered, someone will inform the police."

He laughed. "Empty threats, Miss Brinton. By then we'll be miles away. Aren't you eager to ride across the desert sands with me, lie beneath the stars, with only the winds for company? I'll teach you to appreciate the beauty of emptiness...."

"Oh, shut up," she cried, seeing that his smile was full of mockery. She longed to burst into tears, but determined to show him no weakness.

He knelt down beside her, his eyes holding hers. She was well aware of his primitive magnetism. What could she possibly do if he did make love to her?

# Desert Barbarian

by

## CHARLOTTE LAMB

*Harlequin Books*

TORONTO • LONDON • NEW YORK • AMSTERDAM
SYDNEY • HAMBURG • PARIS

Original hardcover edition published in 1978
by Mills & Boon Limited

ISBN 0-373-02206-9

Harlequin edition published October 1978

# CHAPTER ONE

THE garden of the hotel was dimly lit by coloured lanterns which swung in a faint sea breeze blowing up from the beach below, shedding jewelled circles of red and yellow on the paths, the fringed palm trees and the flower-beds, giving the garden a new fairy-tale prettiness it somehow lacked by day. Now and then, when the wind blew more strongly, the lanterns swung far enough to bring the blue water of the swimming pool alive with shimmering images of colour, as if suddenly filled with exotic little fish. The gay umbrellas beside the pool, their function unnecessary at this hour, fluttered and flapped over their little white tables. The stone terrace running beside the pool was empty. No one sat at a table, no one swam in the bright water.

From the ballroom came the rhythmic beat of a local band, trying hard to imitate Western music but succeeding only in patches, occasionally the genuine echo of their own wailing rhythms sounding like a wraith beneath the regular drum-beats of the modern dance.

Marie had fled from the dance floor to escape the too-insistent attentions of a rather dull young man who seemed unable to recognise polite refusals when they were given. For five days he had haunted her morning, noon and night. She was on the verge of being rude, and had decided it would be wiser to hide from him rather than say the words boiling on her tongue. Discretion, as

5

her father was fond of saying, is the better part of valour.

She leaned on the low stone wall, staring down at the moonlit sea, listening to the low murmur of the waves as they rolled gently along the curve of the little bay, making an ironic background to the insistent beat of the modern dance music. A lighthouse stood on a promontory to the right of the bay, sending out a steady red beam across the water, laying a glimmering red path across the bay which reminded her of the red of a stained glass window. Somewhere beyond the reach of eyesight a ship made a low moaning, warning of fog far out in the distance.

It had been a mistake, after all, to come here. The brochure had promised her a world more ancient, more mysterious than her own, and it had been in search of that that she had flown here, only to find herself imprisoned in her own world of air-conditioning, hot water and fitted carpets, unable to reach the teeming, enthralling secret world she had glimpsed in her visit to the Kasbah. Their visit had been a brief one, closely supervised by a nervous guide who had not permitted them to wander far from the path he chose and who had constantly looked over his shoulder with visible anxiety as if expecting every moment to be attacked. From the main street they had followed, Marie had seen dark huddled alleys leading away into a tortuous maze of tiny dwellings; women in dark veils shuffling away with lowered heads, olive-skinned, striding men moving arrogantly through the crowds, their dark eyes passing over the little huddle of excited Europeans without interest. For a brief moment she had felt her imagination kindle, only to be led away by the guide, whispering to her of unimaginable dangers lurking in the shadows.

Somehow the fortnight in the mysterious desert had become yet another seaside holiday in a luxury hotel, and she was bored with the whole thing. She was tired of carpets and soft beds, expensive food that managed to taste the same every time, the relentless monotony of comfort and idleness. She might just as well have gone to the South of France or even some English seaside resort. It was true that the desert lay there, beyond the town, but the constrictions of the hotel seemed to impose a barrier between it and the holidaymakers. Marie felt as though she were wrapped in transparent plastic, hygienically protected from the dangerous world beyond.

She sighed. Suddenly a voice made her jump, and turning in surprise, she found Mrs Brown beside her, her freckled, healthy face alight with pleasure.

'Isn't this marvellous? Look at that view! Romantic, isn't it? Oh, I'm having such a lovely time here.' The enthusiastic, breathy voice made Marie envious. Mrs Brown and her quiet husband, Don, had never been out of England before and were ecstatic over their trip. They had won two weeks at the hotel in a competition, and could not get over their good luck. After forty-five years of sedate English holidays, life had taken on a more dazzling lustre for them both.

'I'm glad you're enjoying yourself,' Marie said, smiling at her. She liked Mrs Brown. They had shared a seat on the coach trip to local Roman ruins and become friendly over the sand-buried stone columns and broken walls of the old legion city.

'You're enjoying it, aren't you?' Mrs Brown gazed at her curiously.

'Of course,' said Marie, trying to sound sincere.

Mrs Brown's hazel eyes skimmed over the heavy white silk evening dress the other girl wore, enviously guessing at the price of such magnificence. The other visitors to the hotel could not but be aware that Marie was the daughter of James Brinton, the head of a vast electronics firm based in Southern England. Everything the girl possessed was of the same quality: expensive, stylish and worn with unconscious grace. Mrs Brown, on first seeing her, had been nervous of her, but on closer acquaintance had found that Marie was more approachable than her outward manner indicated. Mrs Brown's own blue chiffon seemed to lose its original charm when she stood beside Marie, and the older woman sighed.

'You're so lucky to have travelled all over the world. I do envy you. Don and I have never been able to afford to go beyond England—there were the children to consider. Our Joanne was never a good traveller, even a trip in the car made her sick, and she could never fly anywhere. Mind you, kids prefer the seaside anyway. They never missed anything. But I used to get travel brochures and read them from cover to cover, longing for faraway places. Now that we're on our own we could get away, but somehow we never got around to saving up enough. There's always something we need, a new carpet, a new car ... something more important than a holiday.'

'You must have been thrilled to win that competition, then,' said Marie, nodding understandingly.

'Oh, I was over the moon! My dreams come true.'

'And it's all lived up to your expectations?'

'Oh, yes,' said Mrs Brown eagerly.

'I'm glad.' Marie smiled back at her, trying to imagine

the life Mrs Brown had led, the quiet, busy days in her home with her children, the dreams and excitements of travel always at the back of her mind to comfort her. It was a totally different world from her own. In its way it was as interesting to her as the exotic desert world she had come here to see. What we do not know is always as exciting as a dream. The human mind is never content, always looking out beyond the confines of its surroundings to grasp new concepts, new horizons.

'What about you?' Mrs Brown asked. 'You enjoyed that trip to the Kasbah, didn't you? I noticed how excited you looked as we got on the coach. Mind you, I was a bit nervous, I don't mind telling you. Some of those Arab stallholders looked a bit sinister. I mean, they say there are still slaves in some parts of the Arab world. You couldn't be too careful out here. If you went too far away from civilisation who knows what might happen?'

Marie laughed. 'I think I would rather enjoy getting away from civilisation. I'm sick of drifting in the swimming pool, drinking a glass of mint tea over the tables, driving around in an air-conditioned coach looking out at this world through plate-glass windows ... I've half a mind to go off and explore on my own, find out what it's really like here...'

Mrs Brown looked horrified. 'I shouldn't do anything like that, dear. I mean, you're a very pretty girl. That fair hair of yours makes you obviously European. I noticed some of those men in the Kasbah staring at you in a very furtive way. If I were you, I'd stay where I was safe...'

'Oh, safe!' Marie whirled round and stared down at the moonlit sea, her mind restless. 'I came here to see the desert, the wild, empty spaces of the world, not to eat

French cooking and dance to pop music. I suppose I had a romantic dream, just as you did, Mrs Brown, but my dream was less accessible.'

'I expect you've seen so many interesting places that you're more difficult to please,' said Mrs Brown flatly.

Marie turned back and gave her a little grin. 'I expect you're right. I'm sorry, I didn't want to spoil your fun by moaning.'

'Oh, you haven't,' said Mrs Brown, smiling again. 'Come back into the ballroom and have a dance with that nice boy who seems so interested in you . . .'

'Not just yet,' Marie said quickly, suppressing a shudder of dismay. 'I have a slight headache, actually. The peace and quiet out here is doing me good.'

'I've got some aspirin in my bag,' said Mrs Brown. 'Would you like some? I'll run and get it.'

'No,' Marie said quickly, stopping her with a hand on her arm. 'No, really. A few moments out here in this cool air will do me more good than any pills.'

'Yes, I agree,' Mrs Brown nodded. 'I hate to take pills, myself. Wiser not to. You get dependent on them sometimes. I had to take sleeping pills after my last baby and it was months before I got a natural night's sleep. I never take them now.'

Marie saw her glance towards the brightly lit doors which led into the ballroom, and smiled at her.

'Don't worry about me, I'll be fine. You get back and have a good time. You're missing all the dancing.'

'Well, if you're sure . . .' Mrs Brown gave her a last smile and hurried back eagerly, leaving Marie leaning on the wall, inhaling the night fragrance of the garden flowers and the faint, salty tang of the sea.

Silence seemed to wash back like the waves of the sea. She felt herself slowly relax, her eyes feasting on the plum-dark sky arched overhead, lit by a thousand points of silvery light from the stars, with the lemon sickle of the moon pinned upon it like a diamond brooch.

There was a faint rustle in the bushes below the wall which lined the path leading to the sea. Marie glanced down, but saw nothing. It was probably one of the lean-ribbed, starving cats who haunted the kitchens of the hotel, she thought. She had seen them often and pitied them, scavenging around the waste bins for scraps of food, kicked and berated by the kitchen staff.

She reluctantly turned away. If she stayed out here much longer she suspected that Mrs Brown would send the dull young man out to find her.

As she walked between the gently moving fronds of the palm trees someone leapt out at her. She jumped, giving a stifled cry, but before she could see anything something dark was flung over her head, muffling her scream and blinding her. Hard arms then lifted her like a doll and carried her away. She struggled helplessly, panic flaring inside her. Faintly she thought she heard someone laugh.

Realising the folly of struggling in vain, she lay still straining all her senses to guess where she was being taken. She heard the grate of sand beneath feet, smelt the salt of the sea closer and closer, heard the increasing mumur of the waves. They were going down to the sea.

After a moment or two she realised that her captor was actually walking in the sea—she could hear the wet slap of water against cloth, the splash of feet moving through the waves. What on earth was the lunatic doing? she wondered dazedly.

Suddenly the arms holding her lifted, then lowered her body, and she found herself being placed on something firm. At once, as the hands released her, she began to free herself from the stifling folds of the material. She heard him moving beside her, felt a rocking motion, heard the slap of the waves against wood. Then her wrists were seized and bound together with something smooth and silky.

'Be still,' a deep voice murmured close beside her. 'If you try to escape you will make me angry.'

'Where are you taking me? Who are you?' Her angry words were lost in the heavy material.

'Like all women you chatter foolishly,' the deep voice said with an undertone of grim amusement. 'Be silent now.'

Her mouth was full of dry fluff from the material. Swallowing, she lapsed into silence, listening intently as the boat began to move, the oars rhythmically grated on the iron rowlocks. Inside the cloth she found it difficult to breathe. She grew hot and angry, twisting her hands in a vain attempt to untie them.

Suddenly the boat came to a stop, rasping across sand, bucking to and fro, throwing her helplessly back aganst the wooden seat. Straining her ears again, Marie heard the oars shipped, then movements, the scrape of feet against the bottom of the boat, then a loud splash. The boat rocked wildly. He had got out, she deduced. The next moment she was lifted and carried again through water which splashed and lapped, on to a beach which appeared to shelve steeply, judging from the way her captor walked.

Gradually she grew conscious of a new sound, the rustle of wind among leaves. The sound of the sea faded gently. The arms which held her seemed tireless. Her captor walked evenly, his long legs striding forward, carrying her without apparent effort.

He halted, and she was shifted slightly in his arms. She heard a metallic click, then the slow creak of a door opening. She was carried through it and heard it slam behind her. Then she was flung down unceremoniously upon something soft. Before she had time to think her hands were untied and the dark cloth whipped away.

She lay, blinking, her eyes dazzled by the sudden flaming of a yellow candle, staring up at a dark figure which loomed above her.

He was so tall that she felt she looked a long, long way to see his face. In his white robes, his head covered by a white headdress bound with a gold cord, he was like a towering column, only the face, half hidden by his headdress, to betray his humanity. Narrowed dark eyes surveyed her insolently. He had a lean, olive-skinned face instinct with arrogance, cruelty and pride.

'Who are you?' she asked, her voice husky with alarm. 'Why have you brought me here?'

His hard mouth parted in a mocking smile. 'Who I am does not matter. I was on the beach while you were talking to your friend earlier. I heard you say you would like to see more of Arab life; what did you say—the wild, free spaces of the desert?' His dark eyes taunted her. 'So I brought you here to fulfil your dream.'

Marie sat up, shivering with fear, her dark blue eyes

very large in the oval of her white face. 'You must be mad! How dare you kidnap me like this! As soon as it's realised that I've vanished the police will comb the city for me. My father is a very important man, he'll be very angry ...'

'Ah,' he said softly. 'Your father. How much do you think you would be worth to him? How much would James Brinton pay to get you safely back?'

She stared at him in shock. 'So that's it! You brought me here so that you could demand a ransom from my father? But ...' Her voice broke off as she frowned, thinking hard. 'How did you know who I was? This must have been planned in advance ...'

'How did I know who you were? My dear Miss Brinton, your photograph has appeared often enough in the English glossy magazines. Marie Brinton, heiress to the Brinton fortune, dining out with some handsome and eligible young man ... or dancing, or riding to hounds, or skiing in the Alps ... you are a much photographed, much talked about young woman.'

Vainly she wished she had not gone out into the garden alone, giving this man the opportunity he had no doubt been waiting for ... Her small chin lifted defiantly. 'So you're just a cheap crook looking for a way to make easy money?'

'Not cheap, Miss Brinton,' he said mockingly. The dark eyes flicked over her white silk dress, the naked gleaming shoulders and the proud swell of her breasts beneath the material, half revealed as they were by the low curve of the neckline. 'Neither are you, are you, Miss Brinton? A very expensive young lady, I would guess. For a man who likes soft, useless white-fleshed women you would be a tempting prize. Perhaps I would, after all, get more for you from an oil sheik than from your father?'

She was frightened by the way his dark eyes moved over her body. Trembling, angry, on the verge of panic, she tried to think of a way of distracting him. 'How much are you going to demand from my father, anyway?' she asked huskily.

He gave her an amused, comprehending glance which told her that he had read her motives in asking the question. 'What would you suggest?'

She shrugged. 'I have no idea.'

He grinned lazily. 'Half a million pounds, perhaps?'

'You're mad! Half a million pounds ...'

'I'm sure your father would pay more than that to get you back unharmed.' He reached out a long-fingered brown hand and lifted her chin to stare down into her blue eyes. 'After all, he must be aware that any man who had you in his power would be very tempted to enjoy the pleasures your revealing dress suggests are available...'

'Don't touch me, you ... you scavenger of the streets!' She spat the words out furiously, having heard them used by one of the hotel staff to a beggar who had sat by the hotel entrance one day imploring alms of the visitors as they went in and out.

The phrase seemed to amuse him. The hard mouth curved in a smile of mockery. 'To make that sound truly insulting the words should be Arabic,' he told her, his dark eyes full of laughter.

'Then I wish I knew Arabic!' she flung back.

'Perhaps I will have time to teach you,' he returned softly. 'I think it might be enjoyable.'

'Don't bother!'

'Arabic is a language which makes love a sensuous delight,' he said tormentingly. 'It is full of love poetry. Sometimes of an evening the Bedouin sit around the camp fire and recite love poems for hours, capping each other with apt quotations, while the stars make a steely glitter overhead...'

'You make it sound very romantic,' she said, her eyes held hypnotically by his. 'But I expect it's far from the reality.'

His thin brows rose. 'And I thought you were attracted to the romanticism of the desert! You sounded wistful when you talked of it to your friend on the terrace outside the hotel...'

'You were listening to us all the time,' she said, half to herself, her nerves jumping at the thought of him lurking in the shadows watching her while she thought herself alone with the night sky. She tried to remember what she had said to Mrs Brown, but it seemed so long ago. She had said silly, futile things and this man had listened, no doubt with that sardonic, mocking smile.

'You expressed a desire to taste the real life of the Arab world,' he murmured drily. 'Well, you have your wish ...' He moved away, lifting the candle so that the pale light moved around the room. 'A typical Arab house, Miss Brinton. Delightful, isn't it? Romantic and exciting ...'

Her eyes moved around the tiny, low-ceilinged room, taking in the dirty, crooked shutters which covered the small windows, the low table in the centre, around which were arranged thick cushions, the large tapestry-covered cushions which appeared to form some sort of couch, on which she herself had been flung. There was no other furniture but a wall cupboard in a corner. The walls were plastered but had been given a grimy patina by time, and cracks ran across them here and there. In one crack a grey-green lizard sat motionless, only the filmed blink of an eye betraying that he was alive.

The yellow candle beam rested once more on her face. 'You are the only thing of beauty here,' he said softly. 'You are very desirable, Miss Brinton. I would get a high price for that golden hair of yours, that smooth, unblemished white skin and those blue eyes. They admire that colouring here. Your life in the harem would not be hard; it would be as filled with luxury, as idle and spoilt, as your life has always been. You would merely exchange one indulgent owner for another. The only difference would be that you would learn other arts, more sensuous and infinitely more enjoyable than those of the sports field which you have pursued until now.'

Marie swallowed, digging her nails into her palms, her eyes fixed bravely on his lean face. 'You ... you wouldn't dare ...'

He laughed at that, a look of reckless gaiety lighting his face and making him younger and even more devastatingly attractive. 'If you knew me better, Miss Brinton, you would not fling out challenges in that light-hearted fashion. Has no one ever told you that the Arabs love a challenge?'

'My father will pay your ransom, anyway,' she said shakily. 'You wouldn't get more ... any other way ...'

He rubbed his chin thoughtfully. 'I wonder ...'

'He will,' she insisted.

He inspected every inch of her again, from her bare

shoulders, along the close-clinging silk of the white gown. 'Yes,' he murmured, 'I think he would.'

She felt sick relief in the pit of her stomach. 'M-may I have some water? I'm so thirsty . . .'

For a moment he did not move, his eyes lingering on her face. She looked at him nervously through her lashes. 'Please . . . water . . .'

He moved away to the cupboard. She watched his dark shadow stalk across the wall, the hawk-like profile sharply black against the yellow light. He found a glass and a jug of water, came back towards her, poured water into the glass and handed it to her. Their fingers touched briefly in the exchange, and Marie felt herself shiver. She sat up and sipped, then slowly rose as if to give him back the glass. As he bent to take it from her, she flung the rest of the water into his face.

He swore under his breath, his hands going to his eyes, blinded by the cold sting of the water.

While he was preoccupied she darted to the door behind him, wrenched it open and stumbled out into a dark alley. She ran, holding up her long skirts, doubled round a corner and stopped dead, finding herself in one of the crowded bazaar streets, lit by smoking flares beside stalls and noisy with the calls of the stallholders as they tried to attract attention.

Her appearance immediately attracted notice. Within seconds she was surrounded by a crowd of excited Arabs, all shouting at her, some of them touching her silk gown or the gleaming whiteness of her bare arms with grimy fingers, exclaiming over her, while others babbled at her in pidgin English, trying to sell her souvenirs or offering to guide her back to her hotel.

She was terrified, trembling, completely hemmed in and unable to escape. 'Please,' she asked, turning to one of the older men in appeal, 'will you take me to the Marina Hotel?'

'Yes, lady, yes,' he said eagerly, beginning to quote a price to her.

But then a voice spoke behind them all, in fierce hard Arabic, and the men fell back in silence, backing away from her.

With a feeling of dream-like inescapability Marie saw the white headdress, the gold cord, the hawk-like face. He grasped her by the elbow and shook her, barking angrily at her. 'Silly little fool!' Then he spoke again in Arabic, his face glaring down at her. The crowd, watching from a distance, their faces curious, began to laugh. One of them shouted something to him, and the others roared in wild amusement. Marie looked round, bewildered and frightened.

The hard arms lifted her again, threw her over his shoulder like a sack of coals, and while she lay helpless in this undignified posture, she was enraged and humiliated to feel a hard slap across her bottom. Kicking and struggling, she seethed as he strode back into the darkness of the alleys while the other men cackled with delighted laughter behind them.

A moment later he carefully locked the door and then flung her back upon her sushions.

'You ... you bastard!' she seethed. 'You enjoyed that!'

He grinned, showing those hard white teeth. 'Yes,' he agreed shamelessly. 'And you deserved it.'

'What did you say to them?' She was sore where he

had hit her, and rubbed herself self-pityingly, although it had been her pride which had been most hurt. There had been something so humiliating about the way he flung her lightly over his shoulder and slapped her. She had felt suddenly like a naughty child, a toy in the powerful hands of this dark-visaged stranger. At that moment the full realisation of her helplessness had come home to her.

'I told them you were my woman who had run away from me. They advised me to beat you and then make violent love to you. They assured me such treatment would be certain to make you more malleable in future.' He gave her a taunting glance. 'I've followed one half of the advice. Perhaps I should now follow the other?'

'If you touch me I'll scream,' she muttered in impotent rage.

He laughed. 'Empty threats, Miss Brinton.' He knelt down beside her, his eyes holding hers, and a wave of weakness swept over her. He had a magnetic strength, a primitive personal magnetism, which made her suddenly deeply aware of her own weak femininity, and his physical power. What if he did make love to her? What could she do?

'How long are you going to keep me here?' she asked, again trying to distract him. 'When news of my disappearance gets out, some of those men in the bazaar will put two and two together. There'll be a reward, no doubt. They will inform the police and this district will be thoroughly searched.'

'By then we will be safely miles from here in the heart of the desert,' he said coolly.

Her heart sank. 'In the desert?'

He gave her a mocking smile. 'I thought you longed to

see the desert. Aren't you eager to ride across the empty sands with me, lie beneath the stars, wrapped in my burnous, with only the wind for company? I will show you the great wastes of sand and sky, teach you to appreciate the beauty of the emptiness...'

'Oh, shut up!' she cried bitterly, seeing that his smile was full of wry mockery.

He laughed, pushing back his white headdress to expose thick sleek black hair. 'You are contrary, it seems, Miss Brinton. Are you tired of the excitements of Arab life already?'

She longed to burst into tears, but determined to show him no weakness. She sensed that any hint of fear would make him despise her, so she had to pretend to a courage she did not possess.

He moved away, searched in the cupboard and came back with a long woollen garment like a tent. 'Put this on...'

'Why?' she asked dubiously, eyeing it without favour. It was a grey-white colour, crudely woven and shapeless.

'Miss Brinton, don't argue. Put it on. If you do not obey me instantly whenever I give you an order I shall be forced to render you unconscious, and I am sure you would not wish me to do that.'

She stared into his face, finding it as grim as carved stone, the dark eyes unyielding.

Reluctantly she lifted the garment and let it fall over her head and down to her feet. Inside it she was very warm. 'I feel like a tent,' she said sullenly.

He grinned wickedly. 'You look like one. No man will look twice at you now.' He put a hand to the back of the garment and lifted an all-enveloping hood over her head so that only part of her face could be seen. 'Now! You could be any Arab woman.'

'Thanks a lot!'

He laughed. 'You sound like a sulky child.'

'I detest you,' she muttered under her breath, half afraid to let him hear.

His strong fingers gripped her wrist. 'Come,' he said. 'We must leave now. The desert night is cold. You will be glad of your tent-like clothes later.'

He led her out of the back door into a close-set palm grove and along a winding path to the back of a low stable. An Arab boy in a dirty white djibbah sat on the floor asleep, his bare heels together, his legs loosely crossed. He jumped up, blinking sleepily, as they approached.

Speaking in Arabic, her captor gestured to the stable. The boy nodded and darted inside. Marie heard the jingle of harness, the stamp of horses' feet. After a few moments the boy led out two horses, saddled ready for a journey. She was lifted on to one of them, a fine spirited little white mare. For a moment she thought of galloping away to escape, but her captor read her thoughts and gave her a cool, tormenting grin.

'I would catch you up in two minutes, Miss Brinton,' he said softly. 'And I would beat you with my riding crop until you begged for mercy.'

She glared at him from below the hood of her garment, saying nothing.

He laughed and leapt into the saddle of the other big black horse with a grace and agility which she could not help admiring. Devil though he was, he had a physical appeal she could not resist. She had always admired men who rode well.

They rode away under the sweeping fringe of palms leaving the boy staring after them. There were a few scattered houses on the outskirts of the little town, most of them surrounded by palm trees, a sandy road running between them and winding out inland towards the darkness of the desert.

'We shall ride towards Wadi Aquida,' he said.

Marie was surprised that he should name the place to her, but already she knew him well enough to guess that knowing the name would be of no help to her anyway.

The moonlight showed her an emptiness ahead, an emptiness so bleak and yet so beautiful that it took her breath away.

The horses rode silently over the soft, flat sand. The cool night air was gentle on her face, blowing through her loose garment and refreshing her. The moonlit sand seemed without shadows so that there were no landmarks for her to pinpoint. She wondered how he knew which way to go. The horses occasionally snorted, the saddles creaked. To the east she saw the dark outline of a low line of hills, and once the horizon was specked by a small ring of palm trees circling a gleam of water, lit by the smoky flame of a camp fire.

'Bedouin!' he remarked, nodding as he saw her stare in that direction.

She was growing tired. They seemed to have been riding for so long, and she was longing for her bed. Her back ached, her hands were icy cold on the reins.

Suddenly she saw a swelling ridge ahead which seemed

to have sprung up out of the ground. They were riding straight towards it, and soon the horses began to climb it, their feet slipping and sliding on blown sand.

As they crested it, she saw another ring of palm trees and the faint, illusory gleam of water under the moon.

'Wadi Aquida,' he said, riding down towards it.

When they reached the palm trees Marie saw that the sand around the water was well trampled, and a kicked-out camp fire still smouldered. For a moment her captor squatted, studying the ashes. Then he looked at her calmly.

'Bedouin. They probably left here an hour ago—the ashes are still warm. Find some scrubwood.'

'I'm tired,' she said sulkily, sinking down beside the fire and extending her frozen hands towards the faint warmth which still came from it.

He bent and jerked her to her feet, shook her like a rag doll. 'Do as you are told!'

'My back aches and I'm stiff,' she muttered, on the point of weak tears.

'We are all tired,' he said. 'The horses need watering. Find as much wood as you can and get that fire going again ...'

Marie stumbled away and began to search under the date palms. She found a few branches of thorn trees, withered and dried by desert suns, and hurried back to feed the fire with them, blowing on it and watching it anxiously. After a while she managed to get a few sparks, then a little flame, then eventually a blaze, which she continued to feed with thorn sticks until the fire was adequate. Wrapped in her loose, warm garment she sat beside it, huddling like a child at the hearth.

Meanwhile he had watered the horses, fed them from the saddle bags and then he moved towards the fire, a battered old iron pot in his hand.

'Fill this from the pool,' he ordered.

She reluctantly stood up and took the pot, returning to the gleaming water with it, filled it and went back to him. He had produced two tin mugs, a flat loaf of Arab bread and some oranges from the saddlebags. He thrust the pot of water into the edge of the fire with a practised hand.

'We'll have coffee soon,' he told her. 'Sit and eat.'

She looked at the unleavened bread with a grimace, but when he had wrenched it into two halves and handed her one, she found the taste quite appetising, hunger being an excellent sauce. She ate two small oranges as well and began to feel much better, although sleepiness was becoming a nightmare to her. Her head kept nodding down upon her chest. She had to force herself to stay awake, afraid to sleep. The warmth of the fire was so comforting that she longed for sleep with an almost passionate longing.

When he had made strong, black coffee he poured her a cup. 'It is unsweetened,' he warned her.

Marie cupped her hands around the mug, enjoying the warmth of it, and sipped, scalding her mouth.

He laughed as she spluttered over it. 'Good coffee?'

Warily she sipped again. 'Very good,' she said, suppressing a yawn.

He crouched beside her in the smoky firelight, his face carved into strange, disturbing hollows, the high cheekbones and ascetic lines of the face emphasised by the shadows around them.

'Sleep now,' he said, taking the empty mug from her. He laid a woven mat on the sand, taken from the back of his black horse. 'You will find this comfortable enough.'

She slowly lay down, watching him nervously as he walked away out of the firelight, his back as straight, his walk as steady, as if he had not spent the night riding across the desert.

Her lids began to flicker, to sink. She listened to the singing of the thornwood on the fire, the soft sifting of ash in the desert wind.

Another sound brought her suddenly awake. A muffled slithering across the sand ... her eyes moved nervously around the fireside ... then she gave a scream, freezing immediately afterwards. A small black snake was lying close beside her, forked tongue quivering on the air, one eye watching her.

'What is it?' He had spun round from where he was attending to the tethered horses under the palm trees.

'A snake,' she whispered, not taking her eyes off the ghastly thing.

'Don't move,' he said, slowly coming back towards the fire. 'What colour is it?'

'Black,' she whispered. 'Very small and black.'

He swore under his breath, adding again, 'Don't move an inch. Don't even breathe.'

She lay rigid, her eyes fixed on the snake. It suddenly began to writhe towards her with an undulating slowness that terrified her. Then there was a deafening explosion and the snake was in two bits—blown into half with one shot.

Marie leapt up then and broke into scalding sobs, shaking from head to foot.

He pulled her into his arms, one hand on the back of her head, pressing her close against him. She wept softly, trembling like a leaf, clinging to him.

His hands moved against her back, stroking her calmingly, soothing her, while he whispered consolation. 'It's all right, it is dead. You were very brave. It's all right now. It can't hurt you now ...'

'It ... it was so silent,' she whispered. 'It ... slithered towards me ...'

'They come in search of the warmth,' he said gently. 'Sometimes they get into your blankets during the night. You have to search the ground before you get up. But there's no need to be afraid. I'm used to them.'

'Are they poisonous?'

'Very,' he said bluntly.

She raised her head, shuddering, but laughed helplessly. 'Oh, you're so damned honest! Why couldn't you lie to me?'

He pushed the hood back from her hair, his fingers lingering on the gleam of gold which framed her white face. 'I'll lie to you if you want me to, Miss Brinton ...'

A slow, warm sweetness was spreading through her body. She hung in the shelter of his arms, relaxed to the point of physical collapse, aware in every nerve of the hardness of his body against hers, the muscled easy strength which had carried him through these last hours of hard riding across difficult terrain yet left him still unwearied at the end. Her own physical exhaustion, coupled with the recent shock and the insidious warmth of the firelight and his closeness, made her head swim.

She looked up into the enigmatic dark face, her smile wry. 'You'll lie anyway, no doubt. After all, what do I know about you? I don't even know your name. I only know you're some sort of kidnapper. You saved my life just then and I'm grateful, but it was you who put me in danger in the first place.'

'My dear Miss Brinton,' he murmured mockingly.

'Don't keep calling me that!'

'What shall I call you?' he asked at once. 'Marie ...' He said the name with soft pleasure, dwelling on it in a musical voice which sent shivers down her spine.

'If you wish,' she shrugged with a pretence of indifference. 'What shall I call you?'

He looked into her eyes thoughtfully. 'The Arabs call me Khalid.'

Her curiosity was aroused. 'What do other people call you? Or wouldn't it be polite to ask?'

He grinned. 'The desert Bedouin have a saying ... a woman stabs with her tongue or with her eyes ... It fits you well, Marie.'

'If I had anything else to stab with I would use it,' she said tauntingly.

He laughed. 'I believe you.' He released her and moved a hand down his white clothes, producing a curved damascene dagger which glittered wickedly in the firelight. Offering it to her gravely, he bowed.

She took the weapon, feeling a helpless rage. He knew she would not use it. It was useless to her out here in the desert. If she did kill him she would never find her own way back to safety; she would die out here of exposure or be captured by nomad Bedouin.

She threw the weapon away, watching the bright arc of light as it fell. 'You know I can't use it. You were quite safe to give it to me.'

'True,' he agreed smoothly. 'Now find it and bring it here to me.'

'Find it yourself!'

He gripped her shoulders with two hard hands, staring down into her uplifted face with compelling eyes.

'Find it.'

Fear leapt up inside her. She knew that stony, commanding face. When he released her she angrily moved away to pick up the dagger and bring it back to him. He took it from her and slid it back into concealment among his clothes.

'Now, sleep,' he said calmly.

Marie lay down, facing the fire, and curled round to sleep again. Gradually her nerves stopped jumping and she felt a deep sleep dragging her down to oblivion. Just on the point of submersion, she became aware of him settling down beside her on the rug. Her eyes warily flicked open and found his face close beside hers, the dark eyes watching her.

'Go to sleep, Marie,' he ordered with dry amusement. 'I have no interest in a forced lovemaking.'

She felt hot colour run into her cheeks. Slowly her eyes closed again, but she lay listening to the regular sound of his breathing, aware of every move he made, every breath he drew. She wondered what it would feel like if... then she jerked herself away from that thought, hating herself for entertaining it for a second. Despite herself, she risked another look at him. He was still watching her as attentively as before.

'What now?' he demanded instantly. 'Are you disappointed that I've made no attack upon your virtue, Miss Brinton? Of course, if you insist ...' The dark eyes mocked her. 'I can force myself to make love to you if you cannot sleep until I have ...'

'Can't you sleep on the other side of the fire?' she demanded. 'You make me nervous.'

He rose suddenly and began to kick out the fire. She watched him, baffled and alarmed.

Then he turned and jerked her to her feet, pulled back the long golden strands of her hair until her face was exposed to him and bent his head. Marie gasped helplessly as the hard mouth silenced her, parting her lips and filling her with a totally new realisation of her own femininity. The hands holding her were fierce and remorselessly compelled her submission, bending her backward so that her head spun and she was dizzily forced to cling on to him or fall. The kiss deepened, grew hot and demanding. Her closed eyes seemed dazzled by an explosion of brilliant light. She knew she was kissing him back, she felt the hot response of her own senses, but she was too helpless to fight, overwhelmed by new sensations. No man had ever made her feel so weak, so female, so much at the mercy of a superior strength. One part of her was furiously angry, scornful at herself for weakly submitting, the other was almost rapturous, glorying in the way he made her feel.

Suddenly she was free. He moved away. Dizzily she stared after him as he collected up the various objects strewn about the sand. He packed them all away into the saddlebags, then returned and lifted her on to the back of her horse.

'Where are we going now?' she asked despairingly. 'I'm too tired to ride any further.'

'We're going back,' he said tersely, mounting. 'We should be there soon after dawn.'

She was incredulous. 'Back?'

'To your hotel,' he said grimly, wheeling his mount away and galloping towards the sandy ridge behind the oasis.

Marie stared after him, disbelief freezing her for a moment, then she followed. When she caught up with him she stared sideways at the enigmatic hawk-like profile.

'Why?' she asked very quietly. 'Why have you changed your mind?' Was it because of their lovemaking just now? she wondered. Had he softened towards her? Or was he sorry for her? Why had he changed his mind?

He didn't answer, riding hard, his gaze fixed on the sky. She rode in silence beside him, hardly conscious of the ache of her back, the weariness in every limb.

'I won't tell anyone about this,' she offered meekly a little while later. 'I won't tell the police anything. I'll say I went out riding alone and got lost.'

He glanced at her briefly then, his face unreadable. 'Perhaps we both got lost,' he said ambiguously.

'What do you mean?' she asked, her face doubtful.

He shrugged. 'It doesn't matter.'

They rode on, across the moonlit sand, and then in the growing greyness of dawn they came in sight of the little seaside resort, with its palm trees and outlying mud-walled houses whitewashed by the sun. They passed into the outskirts, skirted a palm grove and were back outside the little stable. The same Arab boy sat sleeping beside the wall. He got up, rubbing his eyes, held the horses while Khalid lifted her down.

Her legs collapsed beneath her, she sagged against him, so cramped and tired that she could not stand.

He lifted her into his arms again, and she cradled her head against his strong chest with a thankful sigh. For a second or two he looked down into her pale face.

'Allah knows why I am giving away the prize of a lifetime,' he said softly. 'You are as beautiful as the sunrise.'

She flushed, touched by the compliment. 'Thank you.'

He carried her down through the palms to the beach, where the small boat lay beached out of the curling waves. Marie lay sleepily watching him as he rowed along to the other end of the bay, marvelling at his ability to look as if he had just got out of a bed after eight hours' sleep whereas in fact he had been physically working all night, riding across the desert.

When they reached the beach below the modern, palm-fringed hotel, she said quickly, 'Leave me now. I can get into my room without being seen, perhaps, and it would be better if you weren't seen.'

He nodded and watched her clamber out, lifting her skirts clear of the water, then walking slowly up on to the sand.

She glanced back, half reluctant to leave him. He had pulled his headdress down around his dark face, and the dark eyes glinted at her from the shelter of the headdress's shadow.

'If you need money, Khalid, I might be able to help,' she said nervously.

The hard mouth straightened and an angry redness

came up into his face. He looked at her furiously. 'Good-bye, Miss Brinton,' he spat bitterly. 'When I first saw you I thought you a typical product of a decadent society; idle, vain and silly. It seems I was right.' His hands moved on the oars and the boat began to pull away. Marie watched, hating herself for having made such a tactless and stupid remark. Then she turned and walked into the hotel.

She met no one as she padded softly along her corridor. She slid into her own room and sank down on the bed. Presumably Mrs Brown had concluded that she had turned in early because of her headache. There was no sign that anyone had missed her. She guessed that if she had been missed the hotel would be swarming with police.

She took off the looose white garment Khalid had given her and laid it carefully over a chair, then slid out of her white evening gown and went into the shower. The warm water fell on her like desert rain, refreshing and reviving her. She put on a brief, transparent lacy nightgown and dropped into bed.

As sleep overcame her she briefly wondered if the events of the night had been a dream. They faded into sleep, a sleep in which she lay once more beside a desert campfire in Khalid's arms and sank into the delirium of his kiss without a second's hesitation, unshackled by the barriers of class or race, moving to claim him with the freedom and certainty a dream confers upon the human mind.

She did not want to wake up.

# CHAPTER TWO

It was raining as they drove away from Heathrow. Cold, grey spears lashed down around the car with a relentless ferocity which made Marie shiver. After the heat of the Arabian sun England seemed unbearably chilly, a colourless land of leaden skies and mournful landscapes. She thought of the oasis at Wadi Aquida; the flamelit palm trees and glimmering moon-reflecting water, and a curious pain began to ache around her heart.

'Something wrong?' James Brinton asked gently, looking sidelong at her, one hand touching hers as it rested on her lap.

She smiled at him. 'No, just the weather...'

'Good old English weather,' he grinned. 'It always comes up trumps! Every continental holiday I've ever had I've come back to find weather like this—laid on specially, I suspect.' He was a small man, his silver hair brushed to cover the balding spot at the front of his head, his grey eyes quietly reflective. He had built up his firm from a small affair started by his father between the two world wars to a giant which was spreading across Europe at an alarming rate. Sometimes his harassed expression made his daughter afraid that James Brinton was a man who had lost touch with reality—his firm was growing too fast, beyond the grasp of one mind.

'You look tired, Dad,' she said, her expression anxious as she surveyed him.

'I've just been to see your mother,' he replied grimly, his eyes on the rain-wet windows.

'Oh.' She bit her lip. Her parents had been divorced when she was in her teens. Her beautiful blonde mother had eloped without warning with a South American millionaire, leaving a brief note for her husband. Marie had cried in secret, but in public had affected an indifference which had gradually become second nature to her. From time to time her mother reappeared in London, always looking incredibly young and beautiful, draped in expensive furs and dripping with diamonds, her eyelashes fluttering madly every time an attractive male passed by, bringing armfuls of ludicrously inappropriate presents for Marie. Once it had been a large doll which talked in three languages. Another time it had been a party dress four sizes too small. Her mother persisted in believing that she was still a little girl long after she had grown up. Marie had protested about this to her father, only to see him smile a little sadly and say 'My dear, your mother is terrified of growing old. While she can believe that you're still a little girl, she can believe that she's still young. Once she's forced to admit that you're a young woman she'll age mentally, and that will destroy her.'

She thought of this conversation now, watching her father's face. Did he still love her mother? He seemed to have a sensitive insight into the workings of her mind, anyway, and he had never betrayed any bitterness or hatred towards her in Marie's memory. He always saw his ex-wife when she came to England, but he gave no indication of his feelings normally, and she had no idea how he felt about her.

'She wants to see you tonight,' James Brinton added quietly without looking at her.

Marie grimaced. 'Must I?'

'She's your mother,' her father said gently.

'Whenever she remembers the fact,' Marie said with bitterness and clarity.

'All the same I think you must see her,' said James Brinton with a loving glance. 'Try to be kind to her, Marie.'

Something in his tone made Marie stare at him. 'Why? What do you mean?'

'Her husband is dead,' said James Brinton carefully.

'I see.' Marie remembered the large, perspiring cheerful South American without fondness.

'His sons have inherited everything,' James Brinton added without expression.

She almost laughed. 'Oh, no! So that's why she needs some kindness? She's lost the fortune she expected to inherit!'

'I don't like to hear you talking like that,' her father said at once. 'I want you to be kind to her. She's very upset.'

'Upset? Not because her husband is dead but because she doesn't get the money after all!' Marie said bitterly. 'How long is it since I last saw her? A year! And since then I haven't had a letter, not even a postcard. Did she remember my birthday? Did she send me a Christmas present? You know she didn't. **Dad,** why on earth should I feel anything for her?'

'I don't know any reason why you should,' he said gravely. 'It's harder for you to forgive her than it is for me, I realise that. A child always feels more strongly about such a desertion. But she's still your mother and she's unhappy, whether you recognise the validity of her reason for being unhappy or not. Marie, you're old enough to know that no human being is perfect. Your mother was never a maternal woman. She was terrified of having babies. She was always terrified of growing old. You were a sort of index by which others could calculate her age. After all, a young woman who has a twenty-year-old daughter can't be thirty-five, can she? She was never a real mother to you, I know, but if you can be adult enough to forget that, she could still be your friend. And she needs a friend at the moment.'

'Oh, Dad! Why are you so saintly?' Marie laughed, close to tears.

'Perhaps because I realise that I should never have married Clare in the first place,' he said. 'I was always older than she was, not just in years but in mind. She wanted parties, dancing, a host of admirers. I was engrossed in the business, building it up and expanding everywhere. I had no time to squire her around every night. So I just ignored the problem and let her do as she pleased. Of course, we drifted apart. When she left me it was only the inevitable outcome of our incompatibility. I felt responsible, in a way. I talked her into marrying me. Clare always had doubts, but I steamrollered her into marriage.'

'You must have loved her very much, Dad.' Marie felt half embarrassed at these revelations.

'I was crazy about her,' he admitted with a little grimace of self-derision. 'I couldn't rest until I'd persuaded her to marry me. Then, of course, I turned back to my work and left her to get on with a life she had never really wanted. She just wasn't cut out to be a dutiful wife and mother. She wanted the glamour of high society, and she got it in the end.'

'And now she's lost it,' Marie said thoughtfully.

'That's why she needs your help,' he said, patting her hand. 'Be a good child. Go to her tonight—have dinner with her at her hotel. Listen to her troubles and try to be sympathetic. Try to see her, not as your runaway mother, but as a complete stranger. If you do, I think you'll find her charming and pathetic, a lost little girl in a hostile world.'

'Dad, you're still ... fond of her,' she said in a smothered tone of wonder.

He smiled faintly. 'You sound surprised. Perhaps you're not as grown-up as you think, my dear.'

The car drew up at their block of flats. While the chauffeur struggled with the luggage, Marie and James went up in the lift to their penthouse, talking now about Marie's holiday. James laughed at her confession of boredom.

'I'm afraid you're spoilt. Tired of luxury hotels indeed! What would your reaction have been if you'd arrived to find you were expected to sleep in a filthy little room with dirty sheets and no sanitation? Which is probably how many of your romantic Arabs live in those little mud-walled houses they build.'

'I saw someone building one of them,' she said. 'It was quite fascinating. He was so deft! He made the bricks out of damp mud, patted, then cut the mud into bricks with the aid of a special little piece of apparatus made out of wood and string. It was so quick and simple. They leave them to dry in the sun which bakes them as hard as iron—a cheap method of building houses.'

'Would you want to live in one, though?' he teased her.

She laughed, recognising the justice of his irony. 'No, I suppose not.'

'I don't suppose you ever even went into one!' he said with amusement.

Marie thought of the little house behind the bazaar, remembering the yellow candlelight which had illumined it for her, and a slight shiver ran down her spine. She did not reply. Her dreams had been haunted since that night. A dark face, eyes that mocked, hands that were hard and yet unbelievably gentle ... his image remorselessly filled her mind whenever she let the barriers down. She might have said to her father, 'I did meet an Arab. An Arab called Khalid...' and the words would be threadbare, unable to convey a hundredth of the truth.

She looked around the muted luxury of the sitting-room, with its pale blue carpet, white walls, modern paintings, and deep, comfortable brocade-covered chairs. It was all a thousand miles away from the palm-fringed oasis and the firelight beside which she had experienced the most traumatic moment of her life. The two worlds could never meet. In a strange way, this world was the more unreal of the two.

She was still conscious of a feeling of being isolated, cut off from her old life, as though she had been away for many years instead of a mere fortnight. Everything looked strange.

'Mrs Abbot will look after you,' her father said abstractedly, glancing at his watch. 'I have an urgent meeting at three o'clock, so I must rush. I ordered lunch for you. You didn't eat on the plane, did you?'

'No,' she said. 'It was the usual salad and plastic ham. I suppose you haven't got time to have lunch with me?'

'Sorry. I'm lunching in the board room with MacIntyre and Hamley. We're in the middle of trouble.'

'Oh?' Marie glanced at him in concern. So his grey look and furrowed brow had not merely been the result of seeing her mother again? 'Is it serious?'

He gazed at her in silence for a moment, then shrugged. 'At this stage I can't say.'

'What's wrong? Not another strike?' A strike had crippled one of their electronics factories last year for six weeks, losing them millions of pounds in overseas orders.

He shook his head. 'No. A take-over bid.'

She was immediately intent, knowing how such a bid would worry and disturb him. Although he had originally owned most of the shares in Brintons the rapid development of the past ten years had been fuelled by the sale of shares, and control of the firm had passed out of his hands financially, although he was still managing director and a major shareholder. 'Who's making the bid?'

'The Unex Group,' he told her.

She frowned. 'What do they do? I've only heard the name, I know nothing about them.'

He glanced at his watch again, hesitated, then said, 'They're a multi-national company, partly owned by Arabs.'

She started, staring at him. 'Arabs?'

He nodded, not apparently noticing her expression. 'They have a finger in dozens of pies ... electronics, food, oil, manufacturing ... they actually own a number of English companies. They swallow firms whole, stripping the assets and trimming them down as they go. They're offering my shareholders a price which I doubt if I can match. That's why I must see Hamley for lunch today. I have to ask if the bank can back me if I try to fight this take-over.'

'Surely they will?' Marie was aghast at the idea of her father losing the company he had spent his life building up.

He shrugged, his eyes expressionless. 'We'll have to wait and see.'

'You don't sound very optimistic,' she said anxiously.

'I'm not,' he said, moving to the door. 'Don't worry, Marie. My personal fortune is not involved in this and I won't let you suffer.'

'Dad!' She was blazingly angry at that. 'I'm not my mother, remember! What do I care about the money? By all means use it if it will help you. I can always get a job if things go wrong.'

He smiled then, his face lightening. 'My dear girl, what do you think you could do?'

'I'll think of something,' she said lightly. 'I'm not altogether helpless, you know. I've had a good education and I'm not stupid. You never know, I might even get married one day!'

He laughed. 'I certainly hope so. I want to be a grandfather, you know. Look, I must rush, I dare not be late for that lunch appointment. I'll see you later tonight. Don't forget—your mother expects you at her hotel for dinner at seven thirty.'

'I'll be there,' Marie promised. 'And I'll be sympathetic, I promise.'

He blew her a kiss and left, slamming the front door behind him in a way which was not at all like him. He usually closed doors gently with care. She sensed that under his quiet exterior her father was seriously disturbed.

She ate her lunch without noticing much of what she ate, and her father's housekeeper, Mrs Abbot, clucked disapprovingly over her half-eaten meal.

'You hardly touched a thing. Are you sickening for something? I told you you'd catch something nasty if you went to that foreign place. When my late husband, Stanley, was in Cairo he had trouble with his tummy the whole time. That was during the war, of course. Army food was nearly as bad, he said, and he wasn't one to grumble . . .'

'I brought you back something,' Marie said, as the other woman stopped speaking. She picked up a brightly wrapped parcel from the bureau behind her and handed it to Mrs Abbot, who stared at it with overdone amazement. This ritual was proceeded with every time Marie came back from a trip abroad. She always brought Mrs Abbot a present, and Mrs Abbot always pretended to be taken aback.

Now she turned the parcel over and over, saying, 'You shouldn't have bothered. Why, my goodness, what is it? You shouldn't have bothered, you know. I wonder what it is?'

'Open it and see,' said Marie, as she always did.

Mrs Abbot got as much fun out of the parcel first as she could, pinching it and fingering the corners, trying to guess what it was, before at last she untied the string.

Marie had bought her a little Arab statuette of a cat, about five inches high, carved in creamy ivory, with green gem eyes. Mrs Abbot was crazy about cats and kept two Siamese in her own part of the flat. Now she exclaimed delightedly and thanked Marie several times before she departed with her gift.

Marie watched her leave the room with an affectionate smile. Mrs Abbot had looked after her ever since her mother ran away. She was a kind, warm, caring woman without relations in the world since her own husband died. In her early sixties, she was still active and hard-working, with no intention of retiring, although Marie knew that she had plenty of money invested in a building society for the 'rainy day' she had been expecting all her life. She ran the flat with impeccable skill. Her cooking was plain but excellent. She tended to bully both Marie and her father at times, but otherwise she kept herself to herself, preferring to sit in her cosy living-room at the far end of the flat with her two cats rather than go out or meet friends.

What would we have done without her? Marie thought. Then she walked over to the window and stared out at the London skyline, thinking over what her father had told her.

What would they do if her father lost control of Brintons? Would he be forced to retire from the board? She could not imagine what he would do with the rest of his life if he lost the mainspring of his existence. Despite their close relationship, she had always been aware that Brintons came first with him. From time to time she had minded that, but she had learnt to face facts.

She thought of the Unex Group with bitterness. Why were they so greedy, like great sharks devouring everything in their path! The impersonal face of big business hid a cruel ruthlessness every bit as harsh as the bleak wilderness of the desert.

She remembered Ian MacIntyre, chief accountant of Brintons, once saying to her father that it was dangerous to grow much bigger. 'You'll attract the sharks,' he had said. And her father had only smiled and shrugged the warning away.

Marie spent the afternoon on the telephone to her friends, telling them bland lies about her holiday. She would never tell a soul about her night in the desert, she thought, as she hung up for the last time. Let them all imagine that she had spent a blissful fortnight swimming in blue water and lazing on the beach. The reality was a secret locked in her own mind.

For the first time she felt restlessly wistful about her lack of occupation. She had never got a job because her father had insisted it was not necessary. She was supposed to run the flat for him, arranging his dinner parties and lunch parties, writing the personal letters which had to go to friends and doing all the jobs her mother would have done had she not run away.

In fact, of course, she had very little to do all day for most of the time, and filled in the hours with idle leisure; shopping, visiting friends, reading books and playing the piano.

Until now that had rarely bothered her, but now she wished she had a proper job, something to take her mind off the images which continued to haunt her. Every time she relaxed her guard that face flashed into her mind.

Oh, well, she thought, time would solve that problem. In a few weeks she would be unable to remember what he looked like. That time could not come too soon.

She slowly dressed for dinner, choosing her dress with care; a pretty blue dress she rarely wore because of its childlike simplicity, the bodice demurely sprinkled with very tiny white lace daisies, the skirts full and calf-length, swaying around her as she walked. With her hair styled in loose waves around her face she looked like a teenager, she thought wryly, gazing at her reflection.

Well, that should suit her mother. She could hardly manage to look much younger.

Her mother was staying at a large luxury hotel near one of London's parks. Marie asked for her at the reception desk and was immediately directed into the lounge bar. Pausing in the doorway, Marie saw her mother at once. She had hardly changed a hair. At a casual glance one would have put her down as a woman of thirty-five, but in fact, as Marie knew perfectly well, she was in her late forties. The miracle was accomplished invisibly. Her make-up was carefully applied, her clothes expertly chosen. Her beauty remained intact by some magical act of will.

She turned, as Marie entered, a glass in her hand, and for a fleeting second Marie saw an unmistakable look of apprehension on the flower-like face. The blue eyes widened, the mouth trembled, then Clare raised a hand in greeting, smiling brightly. 'Darling! There you are!'

There were, naturally, some men hovering in vague attendance, their faces wearing the sheepish look Marie always associated with men whom her mother took in tow. But Clare calmly dismissed them all with a few sweet words, saying, 'Darlings, you must run along now. This is a very private meeting...' The smile which accompanied the words left the men bemused as they drifted away.

'You haven't lost your touch,' Marie said lightly, brushing her mother's raised cheek with her lips. 'How are you, Clare?' Her mother preferred to be called that. She said the name Mother was 'ageing'.

'Hasn't James told you? Poor Arturo ... so sad. And those horrible sons of his, grabbing everything, even my cars and my house. All I had left was the clothes I stood up in, I swear.' Clare looked tragic, her lower lip trembling, her wide pansy blue eyes filmy as though with tears.

Marie glanced at the flat pearl studs in her mother's tiny ears; at the diamond bracelet clasped around that slender wrist, at the diamond and pearl brooch discreetly pinned into the elegant black dress into which her mother's slender youthful body had apparently been poured so that it clung to her from the neck to the hem, accentuating the delicate sway of her hips, the alluring uplift of her breasts.

She vividly recalled the other jewels which Arturo had showered upon Clare over the years, and suspected that Clare's poverty was by no means as drastic as she wished people to think.

'I'm very sorry, Clare,' she said, however, mindful of her promise to her father. 'You look marvellous, in spite of your grief...' then hoped her mother would not take the words as irony.

Clare, however, was ready to accept her words at their face value, eager to be friends, apparently.

'Thank you, darling.' The blue eyes scrutinised her,

approving of the blue childlike dress. 'You look very sweet yourself. I like to see you dress your age. I thought, last time we met, that you were in that tiresome stage of trying to be very sophisticated, which doesn't suit the young, you know. What will you have to drink?'

'Something cool and refreshing,' Marie said demurely.

Clare ordered her a glass of lemonade, adding mischievously, 'With just a dash of gin, barman. We don't want to overdo it, do we?'

Marie saw the barman eye her curiously, and lowered her lids. It would become tiresome, she thought, if she had to keep up the fiction of being sweet seventeen for hours. But it was all in a good cause if she was to keep her mother happy and satisfy her father.

After their drinks they repaired to the dining-room to eat. Clare gazed at the menu with glazed despair, then ordered melon and salad. Marie decided to follow suit to keep her company, and was rewarded with another smile.

'Very sensible. You must look after your figure.' Clare studied her with knowledgeable eyes. 'Tell me about your boy-friends.'

Unconsciously, Marie wrinkled her nose, thinking of the men she knew, her escorts in past months: Nigel with his bland smile and passion for cars, Daniel who talked obsessively of cricket and danced like a rogue elephant, Stephen, the shortest man she had ever met, who was aggressively masculine and carried a chip on his shoulder the size of a tree.

Clare saw the expression and laughed suddenly, her eyes bright. 'Darling! I know just how you feel! Dull, are they?'

'As ditchwater,' said Marie.

Their eyes met in a smile of entirely new sympathy. Clare leaned her elbows on the table in an attitude of confidentiality. 'Poor girl! Has there never been anyone who...?' Her carefully pencilled brows rose enquiringly.

Marie, caught off guard, thought of Khalid, and at once her mother's face reflected an amused curiosity.

'I see there was someone. Who was he? Was he exciting?'

Marie laughed ruefully. 'Very.'

'English?'

'No,' Marie admitted.

'No, darling, they rarely are,' her mother mourned. 'Are you still seeing him?'

Marie shook her head, her lower lip caught between her teeth, and Clare's blue eyes shrewdly assessed her.

'Serious?'

Marie shrugged. 'I don't know. But...' words failed her and she broke off the sentence, unable to put into words what she felt.

Clare sighed sympathetically. 'I see—like that. Well, if you want my advice, darling, which of course you don't, but I'll give it all the same ... go after him if you want him. They say men are the hunters, but that's just a myth invented by women to flatter the poor deluded creatures. Of course it's the woman who pursues, but she does it so subtly that he always imagines it was his own idea.'

Marie laughed aloud, and as she did so her laughter attracted some attention from a party just entering the dining-room. They halted to look at her, and she, looking up, aware of being watched, saw her father smiling at her across the room. She smiled back at him, delighted to see him. Then her glance moved on to his companions, and something happened to her heart. She felt a quick fierce pain, as though someone had squeezed her heart in a vice. Her breath seemed to stop and her pulses to accelerate.

For what seemed an endless eternity her blue eyes looked into the mocking dark eyes of Khalid.

Then he bowed, and Clare, who had turned in her chair to see what Marie was staring at, gave a little cry of amazement.

'Why, there's James, and he has Stonor Grey with him. Now what are those two doing together, I wonder?'

'Which one is Stonor Grey?' Marie asked with an effort, trying to silence the thunder of her pulses, her eyes moving around the little group of men who were now advancing towards them with polite smiles. She recognised Ian MacIntyre, a stooped man of fifty with a tired smile, but the other two men were strangers to her. One was in his early thirties, with short curly brown hair and trendy clothes. The other was plump, smooth, cordial, his dark suit cut on fashionable lines.

'Darling, you must have heard of Stonor Grey,' said Clare in scornful disbelief. 'He's the whizz-kid behind Unex; of course, he started with an enormous personal fortune. His mother was the granddaughter of an oil sheik, so he had a lot of money from her, and his father was Sir Ronald Grey, the stationery king. You know, they make paper and office equipment by the billion . . .'

Clare had said all this very fast, very softly, while she

kept smiling towards the men. She had just finished before they joined them, and she extended her hand to Stonor Grey with a charming, eyelash fluttering smile.

'Stonor! How are you?'

He bent his black head to kiss the back of her hand with a courtly gesture. 'Clare, you look as enchanting as ever. What magic spells do you say? You look about twenty-five.'

'Ssh, don't mention age!' she pouted. 'I'm old enough to have a daughter who's nearly grown up ... Marie, this is Stonor Grey. Stonor, my little girl.'

Marie coolly offered him her hand. He took it, turning slightly away from the others, so that only she could see his expression. The dark eyes mocked her as he bent over her hand. The courtly gesture was somehow different this time. As he brushed his lips over her hand he let them slide down until they touched the little blue pulse beating with telltale speed at her wrist.

She was so angry she could scarcely breathe. Rage sent sparks into her blue eyes; made her fingers shake and her lips tremble so that she had to bite at their inner skin to stop them from visibly trembling.

No doubt he thought himself a great humorist. The full situation burst upon her gradually, like a series of wild explosions. He had pretended to kidnap her in order to make her look a fool. All that stuff about a ransom ... carrying her off into the desert for a few hours ... just to teach her a lesson!

'Stonor is an original,' Clare was saying. 'You must get him to do some of his imitations of politicians. He's so funny.'

'Oh, a comedian?' said Marie, her tone involuntarily touched with acid.

Stonor laughed, and Clare looked puzzled, while James Brinton stared at his daughter with anxious bewilderment.

'Sometimes I get carried away with my little jokes,' he said, the dark eyes on her face.

'That can be dangerous,' Marie snapped.

He smiled wryly. 'Very true. I gather you've just come back from a trip to my mother's country, Miss Brinton. How did you like the desert?'

She had a hard job to fight down her first reaction, which was to slap his face. With a great effort she managed to say sweetly, 'The desert was ... sandy, Mr Grey.'

'And the people?' he asked still in the same courteous, detached voice.

'I met some very pleasant people. Only one person seemed at all objectionable.'

'And who was that, Miss Brinton?' he enquired suavely.

She shrugged one slender shoulder, her oval face scornful. 'Oh, no one of any importance. Just one of those silly men who think they're irresistible ...'

Clare gave a soft chuckle, but James Brinton looked astonished. 'Marie? What happened? You never mentioned it to me?'

'It really didn't matter, Dad. I got away from him without any trouble. He was the sort of pest who's so consumed with vanity that he's merely laughable.'

Stonor Grey's eyes were filled with shameless laughter. She saw that, far from having offended or shocked him, she had merely amused him. Gravely he said, 'I hope you slapped his face, Miss Brinton. Men like that have to be taught a lesson. The trouble is, so many girls get taken in and swoon helplessly in their arms. I'm sure you were far too level-headed to be swept off your feet merely by a handsome face and a charming manner.'

She glared at him, silenced by sheer awe-stricken rage at his effrontery.

Her father gestured to the other two men, introducing them to her. 'These are two gentlemen who work with Mr Grey, my dear. Stephen Brent and Henry Carr. My daughter, Marie...'

She smiled and shook hands with them. Stephen Brent was the younger of the two, his hazel eyes pleasant, his smile admiring.

'As you seem to have finished your meal, may I suggest you join us and drink your coffee at our table?' suggested her father.

Clare cheerfully agreed to this, so they moved over to a table large enough to accommodate them all. The men ordered steaks and salad with a purely cursory glance at the menu.

'Are you sure we won't be in the way?' Marie discreetly asked her father as they moved. 'Aren't you here to talk business?'

James Brinton gave a little sigh. His face had the weary grey look which had worried her earlier. 'It's all over bar the shouting,' he said flatly.

She gave him a quick, anxious look. 'What do you mean?'

'Unex will take over Brintons,' he said in the same dull voice. 'Hamley tells me I can't raise the capital to match their offer, let alone outbid them. I'm overstretched as it is. He couldn't help me.'

'Oh, Dad!' She put a hand over his and squeezed his fingers helplessly. 'Not even if you used your own money?'

He shook his head. 'Even if I mortgaged or sold everything I had I couldn't pull if off, and if I did manage to do so by a superhuman effort I would handicap the firm for years to come with a massive burden of debt. The game isn't worth the candle.'

She was stricken, looking at him with miserable anxiety. She could see that this had been a terrible blow to him. His whole life had been destroyed overnight. She looked at Stonor Grey as he seated himself at the table, the lean ascetic face as hard and immovable as flint while those dark eyes were lowered, his powerful body sheathed in elegantly cut evening clothes which disguised the predatory virility of the man in a way which the Arab robes had not done.

He had done this to her father. Like some hawk of the desert he had flown down with cruel talons and ripped her father's life to pieces for a mere whim.

Suddenly the dark eyes lifted and met the bitter, accusing glare of her blue eyes. He glanced down at her hand, tightly linked with her father's, and a cool comprehension came into the intelligent face. It was, she thought, impossible to hide anything from this man. His mind was as quick as lightning, flashing into and illuminating the dark places of thought. He would always be able to read her expression. Grimly, she determined to learn to control her features so as to leave him no clues.

While the men ate their meal, Clare talked, sipping

cups of black coffee. She held them all captive, yet her talk was neither sparkling nor witty. Somehow she managed to captivate without effort. Marie marvelled at her ability. Only James Brinton seemed immune tonight, eating dully without interest, his mood too grim to respond to Clare's charm.

A band began to play on a raised dais in one corner and some of the diners got up and began to dance on a tiny wooden floor just in front of the band.

Stonor Grey flung down his napkin and rose. Before Marie had realised what was happening, he had bent and raised her to her feet with one compelling hand, in a grip she instinctively recognised.

'Let's dance,' he said briefly.

She would have protested had she not wished to preserve the peace, but tonight she was afraid to do anything which might further upset her father.

So she allowed him to lead her on to the floor and pull her into a close embrace, his hand warm in the small of her back, while they moved to the deep rhythmic beat of the pop tune.

'Better get it out before you explode,' he murmured drily into her ear.

'What?' She turned her head to look at him and then looked away, her body springing wildly alive as she became aware of his closeness and the touch of his hand against her body.

'You've been sitting there seething for the last half hour,' he said. 'You have a very expressive face, you know.'

'What do you expect? You played a dirty trick on me. You made a fool of me...'

'You were bored, so was I,' he said lightly. 'I thought we might have some fun together.'

'I can imagine your idea of fun,' she snapped.

He ran his hand along the full length of her spine, and she stiffened and glared at him. 'Stop that!'

'Don't snarl at me, then,' he said blandly. 'You were lamenting the fact that you hadn't seen any of the wild, romantic side of Arab life, so I supplied it for you, free, gratis and for nothing. You ought to be grateful.'

'Oh, I am, thanks a million,' she said sarcastically. 'You scared me out of my wits, you made me ride for miles across a barren desert, kept me up all night and told me a string of ridiculous lies ... and you expect gratitude!'

He laughed softly. 'Come on, admit it. You had the time of your life. Wasn't it romantic? The desert, the moonlight, the campfire?'

'That evil-smelling cloth over my head stifling me, nearly being bitten by a poisonous black snake, riding until my back nearly broke in half ... oh, it was certainly romantic! Like taking a bath in sheep dip.'

His black eyes danced with amusement. 'Scorpion,' he murmured softly. 'You've had your revenge, haven't you?'

Marie looked at him blankly.

'You very thoroughly chastised me in front of them all just now and I couldn't do a thing about it,' he said teasingly.

'Don't lie! You didn't give a damn what I said,' she said furiously.

He laughed again. 'You looked so incredulous when

you saw me! Rather like your expression when you saw that snake out in the desert.'

'Snakes always make me look like that,' she said meaningfully. 'What were you doing in the hotel garden anyway? Why were you lurking about at that hour of the night?'

'I was on my way to bed,' he confessed.

'You were staying in the hotel?' She was astounded. 'I never saw you.'

'I wasn't exactly a guest,' he admitted. 'I own it.'

'I might have known it!' She looked at him with loathing.

'I own a lot of hotels,' he told her. 'I visit them all once or twice. It just happened to be that one on that particular night.'

'Why did it have to be while I was staying there?' she lamented to herself. 'Why not some other night of the year?'

'It is the will of Allah,' he said mischievously.

She looked up at him. 'That isn't how I would describe it. Why were you wearing Arab dress?'

'I'm half Arab,' he said flatly. 'Why not? When I'm visiting my mother's country I always wear Arab dress. Don't you like it?' The dark eyes rested on her face.

'It suits you,' she said, suddenly breathless.

Stonor Grey smiled.

For a few moments they moved in silence, with the harmony of people who habitually dance together, their steps moving easily and gracefully.

Then Marie remembered, and looked up at him. 'You'll kill my father if you go on with this take-over bid, do you know that?'

His face grew sombre. 'You exaggerate,' he said. 'Business is only business.'

'Not to Dad. That firm is his life.'

'Then he's a fool. He has you.'

'He has always put the firm first,' she admitted.

'No man should put his work before his family. People matter more than things.'

'All the same, it will kill him to lose Brintons.'

'I hope not,' he said flatly.

'You could stop the deal,' she said huskily.

There was silence. Marie looked up and found him watching her intently, a curious look on his face.

'Couldn't you stop it?' she asked him in pleading tones.

'Are you asking me to do this for your sake?' he asked in a neutral voice.

She flushed hotly. 'No, of course not. For my father's sake.'

He shrugged. 'Unex controls dozens of firms like Brintons. We took them all over in the same way, and none of their previous owners died as a result.'

'Dad is different,' she said despairingly. 'He ... has nothing to put in its place.'

The music stopped, and the other dancers clapped. Stonor Grey guided her back to the table, his hand under her elbow. They found an argument going on between the other men. James Brinton was flushed, his eyes hot and weary. His voice rose above the others.

'You'll put hundreds of workers out of a job if you close down the Birdley factory. Don't you care about that?'

'It's uneconomic to run the plant,' said Henry Carr

brutally. 'It overlaps with one of our others. We don't need it.'

'Asset-stripping ...' James Brinton ground the word out, rising, one hand at his collar, his breath coming in a ragged, uneven fashion that terrified Marie.

'James!' Clare was at his side, her face pale, staring at him as she tried to catch him.

He made a choked sound and fell forward on to the table. People at a nearby table screamed and the waiters came running, while the whole restaurant rose to stare. Marie ran and knelt beside her father, tears hot in her eyes.

Behind her she heard Stonor say in decisive, icy tones: 'Get an ambulance here at once.'

She looked round at him, white-faced and shrivelled with pain. 'You've killed him!' she whispered hoarsely.

# CHAPTER THREE

His dark eyes looked into hers, the blackness of the pupils seeming to dilate with anger. Then he pushed her unceremoniously out of the way, bent and lifted her father with an ease that reminded her of the way he had carried her through the gardens of the Hotel Marina and down to the moonlit beach. Shouldering his way through the staring crowd, he paused to ask the head waiter: 'Is there a room we can use?'

They were directed to a room on the ground floor. Clare and Marie followed the tall, striding figure, their eyes on his burden with the tension of terrified anxiety. James lay with head lolling back over Stonor Grey's arm, his silvery hair ruffled, pale pink patches of scalp showing through. One arm trailed along behind, the hand curiously, painfully, lifeless, the fingers loosely dangling.

Stonor gently laid him on the narrow single bed in the room, while Clare stood, staring at the still body. She scarcely seemed able to breathe, her hands caught stiffly at her breast in an attitude of terror.

A stir at the door heralded the doctor. He looked at them all impersonally. 'What happened?' As he spoke he was already beginning to examine James, and he cut short Stonor's curt explanation with a nod. 'Right, everyone out of the room now. Where the hell is that ambulance?'

The next moment, it seemed, the ambulancemen were

there, carrying James past on a stretcher, his face covered by an oxygen mask, while the doctor walked beside him.

'I must go with him,' Marie cried, hurrying after them.

Clare stood staring after her, her white face drawn. Stonor laid a hand on her arm and she looked round at him.

'I'll drive you to the hospital,' he said gently.

She nodded, silent and tearless, yet visibly on the point of tears.

Then Stonor moved fast, catching up with Marie, his hand descending on her arm. She looked round at him in anger and shock.

'You can't go in the ambulance,' he said.

'Let me go! Who do you think you are?' She flung him off with a furious gesture.

He caught hold of her again, with renewed force, his fingers biting into her wrist. The dark eyes were flintlike.

'You can't go in the ambulance,' he repeated.

'Who says I can't? You?' Her voice was contemptuous.

'Yes,' he said. The simple monosyllable held her, her eyes fixed angrily on his.

'I have a right to be with him. He's my father.' Her voice had lost some of its certainty.

'I'll drive you and your mother to the hospital in my car,' he said.

'Don't bother,' she snapped. 'I'll take a taxi.'

He ignored the childish retort, turning towards Clare, his hand still holding Marie's wrist. 'My car is in the car park below. Would you like to get a coat from your room?'

She silently shook her head. 'Let's go now, quickly,' she said, after a moment.

'Look after your mother,' said Stonor, turning to Marie, his dark eyes suddenly stern. 'She's very upset.'

Marie looked at Clare with wide, incredulous, critical eyes. Her mother had shown no tenderness towards James Brinton for years, yet Stonor seemed to be implying that at this hour of danger for him, her father was more to her mother than to Marie. Then she realised that Stonor could not know that her parents had been divorced. She looked at him scornfully.

'They were divorced ten years ago,' she murmured in an icy undertone, turning away so that her mother should not hear. 'Dad means nothing to her.'

Stonor looked down into her pale face. 'I know about the divorce,' he said coolly. 'Take a look at your mother, a good look. She's in a state of shock far worse than yours. I don't know what she feels about your father, but I do know she needs help.'

Clare was leaning against the wall in an attitude of dispirited patience, just out of earshot, her eyes on the floor, her lips trembling and bloodless. Beneath the careful make-up her face was deadly white. She seemed to have aged ten years in the last quarter of an hour.

Marie stared at her, then her face slowly flushed. She looked at Stonor with dislike.

'You see?' he demanded.

'Yes,' she said, 'I see.' At that moment she hated him for having realised something to which she had been blind. She moved towards her mother and put her arm gently around her.

'Come on, Clare, we're going to the hospital.' Her

voice was soft as she urged her mother along the corridor towards the lift down to the underground car park. Clare looked at her dumbly, her blue eyes like bottomless wells of pain.

'He's going to die,' she whispered. 'James is going to die. What will I do?'

Over her head Marie met Stonor's cold eyes. She hugged her mother and murmured comfortingly, 'No, he's strong. He isn't going to die ...'

Clare shook her head. 'I heard you say I'd killed him ... you said it when he collapsed ...'

'Not you, Clare,' said Marie, aghast. 'I didn't mean you ...'

'It's my fault,' Clare whispered. 'All these years, my fault ...'

'No,' Marie urged, stroking her hair. She hesitated, biting her lip, then said recklessly, 'Dad loves you, he loves you!'

Clare lifted her head then, her blue eyes wild. 'Do you think I don't know that?' Her voice held an agony of pain and self-reproach.

Marie was silenced. The lift purred to a halt, Stonor moved over to his sleek silver-blue limousine, unlocked it, turned and helped Clare into the back. Marie slid in beside her. Stonor got into the driving seat and started the engine.

They sat in the white-tiled corridor staring at a green baize-covered swing door which constantly admitted and expelled a number of medical staff. Above the door a large white-faced clock registered the minutes with a slow, remorseless click as the large black hand moved on. They had been there for two hours. No news had come out. James was in one of the rooms on the far side of that swing door, fighting for his life.

Stonor came back for the second time with coffee in plastic cups. Clare accepted hers without comment, her face frozen. Marie looked up as she took a cup from him. Stonor's eyes were still icy. She knew he would never forgive her for what she had said to him when her father collapsed, but at this moment she did not care. She hated him. She hated everything he stood for: Unex, the impersonal brutal world of high finance, the spiritual desert of business where money meant everything and people nothing, where accountants were masters. She thought of the empty open spaces of the desert, the miles and miles of arid sandy waste. That night beside the campfire she had seen in it a terrible beauty. Now she saw only the bleached bones of its victims, the death and horror of its sterility.

Stonor moved away again. Marie drank her coffee without tasting the plastic, crumpled up the cup and threw it into a waste bin. The slap of feet along the corridor made them all turn their heads. A nurse in clean white apron and cap glanced at them without expression, went through the swing door. The black hand moved on once more with a sharp click.

A tired doctor in a crumpled white coat, stethoscope hanging from one pocket, came out of the door, paused and stared at them.

Stonor rose and moved over to him, speaking in a low voice. Clare rose, her eyes stretched in agony.

The doctor glanced at her, smiled politely. 'Mr Brinton is resting at the moment. I'm afraid there's no point in waiting any longer. No one can see him tonight.'

'He's still...' Clare's voice broke off helplessly, her hands made a pathetic gesture of appeal.

'He's holding his own,' the doctor said firmly. 'That's all I can say at the moment. There's no immediate danger, I assure you. I want you to go home now and sleep. Then you can come back here tomorrow and perhaps by then you may be able to see him.' He looked at Stonor. 'I could prescribe something to help her sleep.'

Clare gestured again, irritably. 'I have sleeping pills, thank you. Never mind me. You swear James is all right?'

He smiled gravely at her. 'Mrs Brinton, he has had a serious heart attack. You must judge for yourself what that means. All I can tell you is that he's holding on ... if the will to live is there, he may pull through. It all depends on him now.'

'The will to live,' Marie said huskily. She looked at Stonor, but his face was mask-like. 'But has he got that?'

Stonor took the doctor's arm. 'Couldn't his daughter see him for a moment? Just look at him.'

The doctor looked surprised, glanced at Clare, who stared at the floor sightlessly.

Marie said huskily, 'No, my mother must go in ... if anyone can give Dad the will to live it's my mother.'

Clare's head lifted. She stared at Marie, her lips shaking. 'Marie...'

'Go in and stand by his bed, Mother,' Marie said softly. 'Say his name. The firm doesn't matter—you do.'

The doctor and Stonor exchanged glances, then Stonor nodded. The doctor hesitated, then said to Clare: 'Will you come with me, Mrs Brinton?'

Clare followed him through the swing door.

Alone with Stonor, Marie sat down again and folded her hands in her lap. After a moment he came and sat beside her, his long legs stretched out across the corridor.

'That was very brave of you,' he said quietly.

'Was it?' Her voice was savage. 'I was only thinking of him. I know he loves her. She may just pull him back. It was a chance worth taking.'

He put a hand on hers, but she pushed him away. 'Don't touch me! You've done enough for one day. Why do you stay here? Why don't you go? I can't stand the sight of you!'

'I'll drive you home when your mother comes back,' he said, his voice level.

'We can call our chauffeur, thanks,' she said.

'I'll drive you,' he repeated expressionlessly.

Marie lapsed into silence. She would not argue with him while her father lay dying a few yards away.

The door swung open again and Clare came out, looking less tense. She looked at Marie across the corridor and her eyes shone with tears. 'Thank you, darling,' she said in a choked voice.

Marie went to her, put an arm around her. 'Was it . . . awful?'

'Awful,' Clare whispered. 'But not as bad as I feared. He wasn't conscious, but they let me hold his hand and his fingers clung . . . his fingers clung, Marie.'

The doctor came out, a smile on his tired face. He gave Stonor a nod. 'I think something got through. His pulse is improving.'

'When can we come tomorrow?' asked Clare impatiently.

'Ring us in the morning and we'll decide then,' the

doctor told her. 'Things take time, you know. We won't
be sure about anything for a long while yet.'

Stonor drove them back to the flat. Clare, without discussion, accepted Marie's suggestion that she come there
for the night. Marie felt she could not leave her mother
alone in a hotel bedroom at such a time.

Mrs Abbot met them at the front door, her eyes pink
from weeping. 'Is it true? Is it true?' she asked. 'Is he
dead?'

'Of course he isn't dead,' Marie burst out angrily.
'Who told you that?'

'The newspapers have been ringing up for hours. They
said he had had a fatal heart attack over dinner at the
hotel . . .'

'A heart attack,' Stonor put in coolly, 'but not a fatal
one, thank God.'

'Oh, thank God, sir, yes,' Mrs Abbot murmured.
'Come in, I'll get you all some coffee . . .'

'My mother would prefer cocoa,' Marie said quickly.
'She must get some sleep. Coffee would keep her awake.'

Mrs Abbot looked at Clare with hostility. 'Oh, Mrs
Sebastian, it's you, is it? I didn't expect to see you here.'

Clare seemed unaware of her hostility. The dark circles
under her blue eyes, the pallor of her face, lent her a new
but fragile beauty. She reminded Marie of a wood an-
emone trembling in a cold spring wind.

She encircled Clare protectively with her arm. 'My
mother will sleep in my father's room tonight,' she said
clearly, her eyes reproving Mrs Abbot.

The old woman flushed angrily. 'I don't think Mr
Brinton would like that, indeed I don't.'

'Thank you, Mrs Abbot,' Marie said fiercely. 'I'll take

my mother there myself.' She led Clare down the hall, her arm around her waist.

Mrs Abbot watched with undisguised anger as the two of them went into James Brinton's bedroom.

Clare looked around the room, flinching as her eyes fell upon a large studio portrait of herself beside the bed. Marie was surprised to see it there. She had not been into her father's room often, and she had never suspected that he kept a picture of Clare beside his bed.

'Mrs Abbot is right,' Clare said huskily. 'I shouldn't be in here. I'll take the spare room.'

'I know Dad would want you to sleep here,' Marie said with a hard certainty. 'I suppose it's silly, but I have a feeling that it will actually help him.'

Clare stared at her, biting her lower lip. 'How can it? I don't understand you, darling.'

'I'm not sure myself,' said Marie, with a faint smile. 'Perhaps your being in this room will give you a tele-pathic link with him ... didn't you say his fingers clung when you touched him, although he was unconscious? How could he know you were there except by tele-pathy?'

'Do you believe in telepathy?' Clare asked her seri-ously.

'I've never thought about it before, but I don't see why not. Anything which would help Dad is worth trying. I just have this instinct ... a vague feeling ... that he would like you to be here.'

Clare sighed. 'Then I'll stay. You know him better than I do, darling.'

'Oh, no,' Marie stared at her in distress, 'don't say that! I only know one aspect of him—he's my father. I don't know him the way you do. You were married to him for years, after all.'

'We lived together for years, you mean,' Clare said bitterly. 'For the first year we were married. Then you were born and after that James never had time for me. From a wife I became just the woman in his house. You don't know what I went through ... I felt stifled, excluded, isolated. When I protested, he suggested that I find a life of my own. Make friends, he said, go to the theatre. He said he wanted me to have fun, but he didn't have time to have fun with me—he was too busy.' She shrugged. 'Any fool could have predicted the end of it.'

Marie turned down the bed. 'Clare, put the past behind you for a while. Lie down, try to sleep. I'll bring the cocoa along when you're in bed.'

'I don't really want any,' Clare said thickly. 'I'll sleep anyway—I have my pills in my handbag. Goodnight, Marie. If ... if anything happens, call me, won't you?' Her blue eyes pleaded humbly.

'I promise,' said Marie, kissing her on the cheek. 'Goodnight, Clare.'

Clare turned away, then stopped dead, seeing herself reflected in the mirror. She put a hand to her cheek, grimacing.

'I look old suddenly. I've always felt quite young, even first thing in the morning without my make-up. But when I saw James choking and dying right in front of my eyes time seemed to rush away from me at tremendous speed. I aged inside. James and I were so young once. If he dies part of me will die too. He's the only one who remembers me when I was eighteen ... you don't know yet, darling, what that means ... but when all those who knew you when you were young have vanished, you really feel old.'

Marie smiled at her. 'You're still very beautiful, Clare. Even tonight ... believe me.'

Clare laughed abruptly. 'You must think me very vain and silly.'

'No, just human,' Marie assured her.

They smiled at each other, then Marie closed the door and went back down the corridor. The kitchen door stood open. She went in, prepared to do battle with Mrs Abbot, and found Stonor there alone, putting cocoa into hot milk and whisking it vigorously.

'Where's Mrs Abbot?' she asked.

He glanced at her over his shoulder. 'I sent her to bed.'

'She had no right to say what she did to my mother,' Marie said.

'You're amusingly predictable,' he drawled, pouring the foaming cocoa into two mugs.

'What do you mean?' She stared at him suspiciously, sensing criticism.

'You fly off at a tangent over everything,' he said, leaning against the wall, his hand propping up his dark head as though he were physically weary. The dark eyes surveyed her, a glint of laughter in their depths. 'Earlier you were angry with me, then you were angry with your mother. You're emotionally unstable. You have to be taught how to respond in every situation. The first angry thought that comes into your head dominates you until you're shown the folly of it.'

'I'm sorry I'm so immature,' she snapped, naturally furious with him at once. 'Perhaps you'd better leave now. I'm sure you don't want to waste any more time on someone so silly and childish.'

He laughed, his eyes mocking her. 'You see? There you go again, leaping down my throat because I tell you the truth. My dear child, you've been both spoilt and neglected. Your father gave you every material possession but never had time for you yourself. Your mother deserted you. But all that's in the past, and now you're an adult. Try to behave like one. Think of things in an adult way. Tonight you've swung back and forth like a pendulum. Once I had pointed out that your mother was genuinely distressed, you were both kind and thoughtful towards her. You became over-protective, enraged because Mrs Abbot was hostile towards her...'

'She had no right to say such things!' Marie burst out.

'I agree, but you see Mrs Abbot is fond of your father, too, and she was just as disturbed by his heart attack as your mother had been. I suspect that your own reaction to Clare surprised her. You haven't always been very friendly towards your mother, have you?'

Marie flushed. 'All right, I get what you mean. I wasn't fair to Mrs Abbot. I'll go and say I'm sorry...'

Stonor caught her arm, looking down at her, shaking his head. 'No, leave it until the morning. I've already spoken to her.'

'Oh, have you?' She was indignant. Who did he think he was, arranging, interfering, ordering everyone around? 'And what did you say?'

'I told her you were too upset to know what you were saying or doing, and I apologised on your behalf.'

'You had no business to do so!' She was very flushed now, her blue eyes bright with anger.

'Blessed are the peacemakers,' he drawled. 'Or don't you believe that?'

'I think you'd better go,' she said.

'Without my cocoa?' he asked tauntingly, sipping from the mug. 'I make very good cocoa, by the way. Try it.'

Marie seethed for a moment, then gave in, picking up the mug and tasting it. They drank in silence, then he put his mug down and looked at her thoughtfully.

'Would you like me to stay the night? I can sleep on a couch quite easily.' His mouth curved in a tormenting smile. 'As you know, I'm quite used to sleeping on the desert sand, and a couch is quite luxurious compared to that.'

'I think we can manage without you, Mr Grey,' she said coldly. 'We have done for years.'

He laughed. 'We can always get along without things we've never had,' he said softly. 'It's custom that makes us dependent.'

'Well, I'm not dependent on you, Mr Grey,' she snapped.

'Not yet, perhaps,' he said, in a softly menacing tone which made the hair rise on the back of her head.

Her pulses raced as he moved towards her, but she lifted her chin defiantly, determined not to show him how his physical presence affected her.

He looked down at her from his greater height, the dark eyes flickering, the thick almost feminine lashes half veiling their expression. 'You look tired, like a little girl. Are you sure you wouldn't like me to carry you to bed?'

'Don't touch me!' she snapped, panicking immediately at the thought of being picked up in those power-

ful arms as she had been before, carried like a child
against his muscled chest.

His mouth parted on an amused smile, the white teeth
showing briefly. 'What are you afraid of? Me? Or yourself?'

'Why should I be afraid of myself?' she retorted scornfully.

'Because you're alarmed by your own response to me,'
he said mockingly. 'I think you're rather inexperienced,
for all your outward sophistication. The packaging glit-
ters, but underneath it lies something far more vulner-
able.'

'You should be a psychologist, not a tycoon,' she said
sarcastically.

'Business requires a great deal of psychological war-
fare,' he said drily. 'Rather like war ... how can you
defeat the enemy unless you understand him? That was
why Field-Marshal Montgomery kept a photograph of
Rommel in his bedroom ... he wanted to understand the
way the other man thought, so that he could anticipate
his every move.'

'Thanks for the warning!'

His eyes teased her again. 'Oh, are we enemies?'

The intimacy of the tone made her feel suffocated for a
second or two. She said flatly, 'Aren't we?'

'There's no enmity on my side,' he said softly.

'There is on mine,' she returned frankly. 'You played a
trick on me, and I haven't forgotten that. Nor will I ever
forget that it was because of the Unex take-over bid that
my father had this heart attack.'

'Your father has had a heart condition for several
years,' said Stonor coolly.

'What?' Marie was incredulous. 'Who told you that?'

'When I do business with a man I like to know all I can about him. I had a report on your father months ago. I knew about his health, his divorce, even about his spoilt, wayward daughter ... when I saw you in the Hotel Marina I had recently read a hefty dossier on you.'

'You sound like the secret police of some police state!' she said in a voice heavy with rage.

He shrugged. 'Information is the raw material of my decision-making process. I never act purely on instinct.'

'Never?' she asked, remembering that kiss beside the campfire in the oasis.

The dark eyes narrowed. 'Almost never,' he conceded, moving nearer, holding her eyes compellingly.

Marie felt a strange fluttering in the pit of her stomach. She knew he was going to kiss her, and for a moment all her instincts demanded that she forget everything, and let him. Then her pride rose bitterly in revolt, and she moved away from him, backing angrily, her glance daring him to touch her.

'Despite what you say, I blame you for my father's illness. Your take-over brought about the attack. If he dies ...'

She stopped on the word, her voice choking, tears rushing into her eyes. She glared at him briefly, then turned and ran down the corridor to her own room and locked the door of her bedroom behind her. As she leaned on the door, sobbing under her breath, she heard the click of a light switch being turned off and then the quiet closing of the front door. He had gone.

# CHAPTER FOUR

JAMES BRINTON continued to fight for his life with increasing strength, helped by Clare's constant presence beside his bed. Marie saw clearly that her father's affection for his wife was growing alongside his return to health. The long, quiet days in his bed were giving him time to think, time to take stock of his situation. He and Clare were happy together, talking quietly or falling silent for a while, learning a new companionship which reaped dividends for James in his struggle with his health.

Marie visited him each day, too, but tactfully left her mother behind when she left the hospital. Clare had moved into the flat fully now, bringing cases of clothes with her. Mrs Abbot behaved towards her with a sort of cool politeness which only just masked a deep hostility, but judging it best to leave things alone for the moment, Marie pretended to be blind to Mrs Abbot's feelings. After all, she thought, there was probably a little jealousy involved. Mrs Abbot had run their home for so long. No doubt she felt Clare to be a threat to her own position in the household.

There had been no sign of Stonor since the night when James collapsed. Once Marie saw some flowers in a vase beside her father's bed, a card from Stonor pushed among them, inscribed in strong, flamboyant writing with his name and a brief message. But she herself had not set eyes on him.

She told herself she was glad.

Several weeks after James collapsed, he came home from the hospital briefly before going away for a long convalescence at a private nursing home. He sat in the sitting-room staring around him in a strangely thoughtful fashion.

'At one time I thought I would never see this room again,' he said. 'Now I realise I never liked this flat anyway. I'm tired of London.'

Marie looked astonished. 'Tired of London?'

Clare smiled at James. 'Yes,' she said to her daughter. 'We were thinking of moving into the country. While James is at the nursing home I'm going to look for a house. Will you help me, Marie?'

'Of course,' said Marie, noting with pleasure the easy way in which Clare was taking charge. 'Where are you thinking of buying a house?'

'Sussex,' said Clare. 'Near the sea. We'll be able to take walks along the beach every day and buy a dog . . .'

'Buy a dog?' Marie laughed and looked at her father in sheer disbelief, trying to see him in this idyllic domestic setting. 'You and a dog taking walks beside the sea, Dad? Are you serious?'

James laughed and shrugged. 'Completely serious, Marie. I've spent most of my life chasing success, making money, building up the firm, then suddenly it all vanished like fairy gold. The business, my occupation . . . gone! Oh, I'm rich enough now, I can do whatever I like. Clare and I talked it over. We're both ready to settle for a cottage by the sea and some peace. Of course, we want you to come, darling. But whatever you think, we've decided that this is what we want, and we're going to do it.'

Marie smiled at him, then at her mother. 'I just want you to be happy. I'm glad if this is what you want.' She hesitated, then asked, 'What about the firm?'

Her father shrugged indifferently. 'Let Unex have it. I no longer care. Perhaps it was time someone else took over. I'd been running the firm for so long, my ideas were getting stale. I was bored with it all, but I didn't even realise that until I came so close to death. Then I got a new perspective on life. I realised that things just don't matter. People are what matter.'

'You're right, Dad,' Marie said softly. 'And I'm glad you and Clare are together again. It seems so right to see you together.'

James glanced at Clare. 'Marie, I would like you to call Clare by her rightful name again.'

For a moment she was bewildered. 'Her rightful name?'

'She is your mother,' he said gently. 'Call her that.'

Marie looked at Clare enquiringly. 'Of course, if she wants me to, but ...'

Clare was pink and half laughing. 'I know I hated it once, but I would like you to start calling me Mother again. You never know you value something until you've lost it.'

'You haven't lost either of us,' James said firmly. 'We're going to be a family again.'

Marie giggled. 'You'll have to get married first, Dad!'

He looked amused. 'I'd forgotten the legal side. I suppose we will. I've never really accepted the divorce, I suppose.'

Clare looked at him half wistfully. 'Oh, James!'

Feeling very much de trop, Marie tiptoed out of the room and left them to discuss the subject alone.

While James was away recovering his strength, Marie and Clare drove around Sussex looking for houses. They saw dozens, but none were suitable. Clare wanted a house small enough to be easy to run, yet with plenty of ground around it to ensure privacy. Just when they were giving up hope of success, they were shown a cottage which had just been put on the market by an artist.

'In rather a ramshackle condition,' the estate agent warned them. 'But basically sound, I assure you. It would cost a little to have some repairs and redecoration.'

Clare sighed and exchanged a look with her daughter. It sounded like another dead end.

The car drove along a narrow marsh lane, winding between ditches and reedy banks, with sheep cropping the soft turf in the fields on either side. The estate agent stopped outside a small blue wooden gate. A crooked sign hung on it. Clare leaned forward to read it and laughed.

'Tom Tit Cottage? How charming!'

Through a tangle of old apple trees Marie saw a thatched roof and faint glimpses of old red walls. They moved to the gate and stopped dead, staring in enchanted silence at the low, rambling little cottage. It was perfect.

'I'll buy it,' said Clare on a breath.

The agent looked taken aback. 'You haven't seen it yet.'

'I've seen enough,' Clare said. 'Enough, that is, to know I want it.'

'I think you ought to look round first before deciding,' the agent pressed her uneasily. 'You'll need a surveyor's report first, anyway.'

Clare opened the gate without taking any notice of him, walked slowly up the narrow rose-fringed little path, which was paved with black and white tiles. A bird-table stood in the centre of an uneven lawn. Blue-tits flew busily around a string of nuts hanging from a tree. Hidden behind high hedges, the garden had a dreamy air, like the garden in a fairy tale. The lead diamonds of the windows glittered in the sunshine.

Suddenly from behind a row of runner beans strung to a string trellis, a head popped up; very short straight fair hair poking out from beneath a wide-brimmed Mexican straw hat, piercing blue eyes and a brown complexion.

'God! I'd forgotten about you coming...' said a deep, horrified voice.

Clare stared, her eyes narrowing. The estate agent smiled uneasily, shifting from one foot to the other, as though his client embarrassed him.

'This is Mrs Cunningham, the owner.'

'Jess Cunningham,' Clare cried in a triumphant voice. 'Fancy it being your cottage!'

The owner came slowly out of her hiding place, staring at Clare. 'I don't think I...' She broke off with a gasp. 'Good lord! It's Clare. Clare Sebastian! Do you mean that you and Arturo are thinking of settling down in England? My dear good woman, you'll hate this place. It's far too remote. You aren't cut out for country life.'

The agent gave a muffled groan of despair, but Clare merely laughed.

'Arturo is dead, Jess,' she said simply. 'Dead three months ago. I'm just getting married again.'

The artist pushed back her straw hat with a gesture of profound amazement. 'Do I know the new one?'

'I don't think so,' Clare said lightly. 'He was my first husband. We're remarrying.'

The artist stared at her in a fascinated silence, then said with a shrug, 'Well, I hope he likes country life, because there's nothing to do around here but paint or catch fish. It suited me for years, but I've just got a commission to go out to India and paint the illustrations for a book on Indian wild life, fascinating stuff. It will take the best part of two years to do the job properly, they think, so I have to sell. Anyway, I think I've had enough of Sussex. When I come home I'll buy a house somewhere more remote—Wales or Cornwall, perhaps.'

'It sounds fascinating,' said Clare. 'Will you show me round the cottage, Jess?'

'Of course. Come along in and have some coffee.'

Clare introduced Marie to her, and Jess shook her hand with a friendly smile. Marie realised that she was older than she had looked at first. Her casual clothes, old blue jeans, white shirt and a vivid green handkerchief knotted around her brown throat, had made her look young, but in fact she was more or less the same age as Clare.

They entered the cottage and went first into the tiny kitchen, a rectangular room with deal panelling on the walls and blue Dutch tiles set into the worktops. Everything was very modern and bright, scrupulously clean.

'This is the only room I've spent money on,' Jess

shrugged. 'The rest I left as I found it. It suited me.'

There were three small rooms downstairs besides the kitchen. One was a square sitting-room, rather dark and old-fashioned, with heavy dark furniture and ornate wallpaper. The second was a tiny room with white walls which contained only an easel, a camp stool and a stack of canvases facing the wall. 'My studio,' Jess said calmly. 'It was originally a larder, hence the white walls. I stripped off the shelves and enlarged the window. It faces south, so the light is good.'

The third room was a dining-room, containing just an oval table and chairs and a large Victorian sideboard on which stood a silver fruit bowl and some candlesticks.

'As you see, it only needs a little money spent on it,' the agent said optimistically.

Clare eyed the furniture with horror. 'It needs a great deal of work,' she said firmly. 'And that's what it's going to get.'

Jess eyed her. 'Going to take it, Clare?'

'Yes,' Clare said certainly. 'I knew that the moment I set eyes on it. The interior is a mess, but the house itself is adorable. I know James will love it.'

'James? Where is he, anyway? In London?'

'He's been ill,' Clare told her. 'Very ill. That's why we want a quiet cottage to live in—James needs some peace.'

'What about upstairs?' asked the agent. 'Shall we take a look up there?'

'Of course,' said Claire, moving towards the narrow, rather crooked stairs with eagerness.

'I'll make the coffee,' Jess Cunningham said. She smiled at Marie and asked, 'Like to help me make it?'

Marie followed her back to the kitchen and helped to get out the cups and saucers while Jess put on the coffee and found some shortbread in a tin.

'How do you feel about country life?' Jess asked her.

'I'm not sure,' Marie confessed. 'Actually, I was thinking of getting a job. I've never done any work, but I think it's time I started. The trouble is, I've had no training at all. I've a sound education, but in the practical sense I have very little to offer an employer. Perhaps I'll learn shorthand and typing.'

Jess turned to study her thoughtfully, the shortbread tin open in her hand.

'Do you like kids?'

Marie looked blank. 'I suppose so. But I couldn't teach—I wouldn't know how.'

Jess shook her head. 'No, I'm not looking for a teacher —just someone to look after Jeremy while I work.'

'Jeremy?'

'My little boy. He's four years old, too young to go to school, but too active to be left in the care of anyone like my mother, who's seventy years old and past child care.' Jess grimaced at her. 'You see, I made the mistake of getting pregnant a few months before my husband was killed in a car crash. I'd barely got over the shock of being pregnant when my husband was killed. We'd been married for years and frankly I thought I couldn't have kids. I was too busy to worry about it much, but Dave always wanted a child, and I was glad for him that I was going to have one. Then he was killed and I had to bring up Jeremy on my own. Out here in the country that wasn't too hard. I looked after him myself when he was a baby. It was easy to paint while he slept in his pram.

Once he started getting about under his own steam it got more difficult, then a woman in the village half a mile away offered to have him for a few hours every day. He goes down to her at ten o'clock and I fetch him back at four, so that gives me a clear working run of six hours. She has two kids of her own, so I think he enjoys it more there anyway. He likes company.'

'Children do,' Marie agreed.

Jess sighed. 'Yes, but the trouble is, what happens when I go to India? I can't leave him behind. I would hate to do that, anyway. I thought I might find someone locally to look after him, but if you would consider the job I would be very grateful.'

Marie stared at her incredulously. 'You want me to look after your son while you're in India?'

Jess nodded. 'You could share our house. They're giving me a house of my own, they tell me. I would pay you, of course. I don't know what the market rate is for jobs like that, but we could find out.'

Marie thought about it and felt a sudden excitement at the idea. She had never been to India. She would love to see it, to live there and be part of the life for a while. Cautiously, she said, 'I've had no experience, you realise.'

Jess shrugged. 'Neither had I had when I had him first. I was a total novice, but I managed. It's common sense, that's all. You just keep him busy and amused all day. Your evenings will be your own, of course—I'll take over whenever I'm not working. There'll be no housework to do because they've promised me someone to do all that.'

'They?' asked Marie curiously.

Jess laughed. 'I'm sorry, I forgot you don't know. I'm

going out there at the invitation of the King of Jedhpur. He's just opened a National Wild Life Park on the plain of Massam outside his capital, Lhalli, and he's paying me to paint these pictures. He intends to publish a glossy book on the subject, and also hopes to sell prints of my pictures to the tourists they hope to attract.' She grinned. 'He's a very ambitious young man. His country is poor, but he thinks they can make money through this National Park.'

'And you'll live out in the park?' Marie was not sure she liked the sound of that. It sounded rather dangerous.

Jess shook her head. 'No, I'll have a house in Lhalli, they say. But there's a stilt house out in the marshes by the river which I can use to do sketches in ... they have it all worked out.' She smiled at Marie. 'Well? What do you think?'

Marie took a deep breath. 'I'll come,' she said.

Jess gazed at her, amused. 'You make decisions as suddenly as your mother!'

'Why not?' Marie said lightly. 'I need a job. I need to work, and I believe in fate. You've offered me just what I was looking for.'

'All the same,' Jess warned, 'you'd better discuss it with your parents before you give me a firm answer.'

'I will,' Marie promised. 'I'll talk to them when they're together. Don't mention it just yet. I'd rather tell them my own way.'

Jess eyed her thoughtfully. 'I see. Just as you say ...'

Clare came down a few moments later, drank coffee, refused a piece of shortbread and had a short discussion with Jess over the price of the cottage. By the time they left the deal was settled. Tom Tit Cottage had changed hands, bar the shouting.

Next day, as Clare poured out the details to James in his room at the nursing home, Marie listened patiently, awaiting her chance to break her own news to them.

When she did tell them, Clare was visibly shocked. 'But you can't leave home just when . . .'

James watched his daughter carefully. 'Why do you want to go, darling?'

'It's because of me,' Clare burst out huskily.

'No,' Marie assured her, smiling at her. 'I'd already decided to get a job before I got back from my holiday. I'm tired of doing nothing, tired of drifting. I want to work, to do something. Jess offered me a change of scene, a chance to do something useful, a chance to learn something about myself and the world . . .'

'But we want you with us,' Clare said shakily, grasping her hand.

James said softly, 'Aren't I enough for you, Clare?'

She looked at him, her blue eyes wide. 'Of course you are!'

'Then let Marie go. She's right—she has been too sheltered up till now. She needs to find out more about life. I've wrapped her in cotton wool. There's a great big world outside there and she wants to find it for herself. It would be selfish of us to try to keep her. Tom Tit Cottage sounds a paradise to us, but to a young girl such isolation would be very boring. Marie isn't ready to retire from the world yet. Her life is only just beginning.'

Clare sighed. 'Very well, James, I suppose you're right.'

'You know I am,' he said teasingly. 'Weren't you

hungry for life at her age? We all have essential stages in our lives. When we're young we need to open out to life. Later on we know what we are and we know what we truly want—then we tend to make our own little place in the world and stay there. Marie has to find her place.'

'I'll always have Tom Tit Cottage to come back to,' Marie pointed out gently.

Clare smiled at her. 'Yes, promise you'll do that, if you ever need us.'

'I'll be back,' Marie promised.

'When does Jess leave?' Clare asked her.

'Next month,' said Marie.

'Then when you've gone to India, Clare and I will take a long cruise to the sun while the cottage is put in order for us,' said James. 'How about the West Indies, Clare?'

'That would be fun,' she agreed. 'But first I must plan the decor and furniture for the cottage.' She gazed at him thoughtfully. 'I think I'll throw all those rooms downstairs into one huge lounge.'

'Not all of them,' James demurred. 'Keep the little studio as an escape hatch. You never know when you'll need somewhere quiet to be alone. I suggest you make the two main rooms into one . . .'

Marie tiptoed out and left them to talk it over. She was filled with excited anticipation of her visit to India. This time she would not be living in a luxury hotel behind safe plate glass. This time she would be living among the ordinary people, sharing their daily lives. She must get some books on the little state of Jedhpur. She had barely heard of it.

A few days later she sat poring over a pile of books,

learning that Jedhpur was an ancient kingdom in the northern hills of India's continent, ruled over by a dynasty of kings descended from a barbaric creature called Jai. The country was mostly mountainous, barren and stony, but there were fertile plains around the river Mas, and it was the Massam Plain which had been turned into a National Park to preserve both animals and countryside from the encroachments of civilisation, and, of course, to attract tourists. There had been some trouble politically over the new park since local farmers had resented the idea, but the King had allowed most of them to continue to farm their land, although it overlapped the area of the park, since they had done so from time immemorial.

The language they spoke in Jedhpur was a dialect, Marie learnt, difficult to comprehend in the rest of the country. English was also used in the capital, Lhalli, for official communications since the King had been to school in England, and some of his subjects had formed a regiment in the British Army before independence.

Clare was with James in the nursing home on one of her daily visits. She had left with an armful of scarlet gladioli, the long sheaves lying against her breast like spears. Together in front of the mirror in the hall, Marie had thought, they looked like sisters. When she told Clare that, her mother had smiled radiantly, the blue eyes childlike with pleasure. Age still held its terrors for Clare, despite her new content.

Mrs Abbot opened the sitting-room door and looked across the room at her. 'I'm just going out to do some shopping. Would you like me to get anything for you?'

'No, thank you,' Marie smiled.

'You'll be in for lunch?'

'Yes.'

'I was going to get lamb chops. Is that all right?'

Marie was surprised. Mrs Abbot rarely consulted her about the menu, despite the myth that Marie ran the household. 'That will be fine,' she said warmly.

Mrs Abbot hesitated. Marie sensed that she was about to ask her something, and looked at her encouragingly. Mrs Abbot took a deep breath. 'Do you think you could take over running the flat if I left? Or do you want me to find someone else to take my place?'

Marie stared at her. 'Are you giving in your notice?'

Mrs Abbot shrugged. 'Things have changed, haven't they? I'm not needed here any more. I thought I'd buy myself a little bungalow down at Southend. I've seen one I like, but I have to make up my mind now, as the owners are in a hurry—they're emigrating, and they want a fast sale.'

'I shall be sorry to see you go,' Marie said gently. 'But you must think of your own future. Of course you must buy the bungalow, if that's what you want. We'll manage. My parents are going on a cruise when Dad comes out of the nursing home, and I'll be going to India, of course.'

Mrs Abbot looked at her, smiling wryly. 'You can never be sure of the future, can you? Out of a clear blue sky something falls wham! And everything falls to pieces.'

'I'm sorry,' Marie said shyly. 'I'm very sorry.'

When Mrs Abbot had gone she lay on the carpet, gazing at the full-colour pictures of Jedhpur; white-capped mountains, brown fields and a winding river running between marshlands rich with birds and animals.

The doorbell rang, startling her, and she glanced at her watch. It couldn't be Clare back already? Or had Mrs Abbot forgotten her key?

When she opened the door she stared in disbelief. 'Stonor! What are you doing here?'

The dark eyes were unsmiling as he surveyed her, leaning on the door-frame with the casual grace which was his birthright.

'I came to see you, surprisingly enough,' he drawled.

'Oh.' For a moment Marie could only stare at him. 'I hadn't expected to see you again.'

'Obviously.' His voice was irritated. 'Aren't you going to ask me in?'

She glanced helplessly back into the sitting-room, littered with open books. 'I suppose so...' She stood back.

'Such eagerness is very flattering,' he drawled, moving past her with an angry glance.

'You took me by surprise. I'm afraid the flat is very untidy this morning.' Hurriedly, with flushed cheeks, she began to pick up the books, wishing she had known he was coming. She would not be wearing dusty pink denims and a short-sleeved white blouse if she had had any idea she would be seeing him. She was angrily aware of her disordered hair, the fact that she was barely wearing any make-up, merely a quick dusting of powder and the palest pink smudge of lipstick.

He bent to pick up one of the books and glanced at it with raised brows. 'Don't tell me you're planning a holiday in India, now? Still chasing the romantic dream?'

She piled the books on the table and faced him, chin defiant. 'No. I'm going out there to work.'

He stood very still, staring at her, frowning. 'Work? You? What on earth do you mean?'

'I've got a job in Jedhpur,' she said carelessly, her pride hurt by his look of disbelief.

'You've never done a day's work in your life,' he said brutally. 'What work could you do?' The dark eyes narrowed. 'And who would be fool enough to employ you?'

'I'm perfectly capable of working,' she said angrily. 'It's none of your business, anyway.'

'I'm curious, nevertheless,' he drawled.

'Then your curiosity must be unsatisfied,' she retorted.

He made a soft sound under his breath, an impatient, infuriated noise. 'Your trouble is that you were never smacked as a child,' he snapped. 'You're spoilt, selfish and impossibly headstrong.'

'That's my problem,' she shrugged.

'I suppose you've given your parents some information about this job?' he demanded. 'They do know about it?'

'Of course they do.'

'And do they approve?'

The blue eyes gazed at him blandly. 'They're willing to let me go.'

'That wasn't what I asked! Do they approve?'

'I think so,' she said lightly. She looked at him between her lashes. 'You haven't told me why you're here. What did you want to see me about?'

Again he made that angry sound, his lips tightening, the lean face taut. 'God knows! I didn't intend to come...' He turned away. 'I'm flying to America tomorrow. I suppose I came to say goodbye.'

'Don't you know?' Unconsciously her tone was provocative.

He swung round, took three strides towards her and caught her by her slender shoulders, glaring down at her. 'No, I don't know. I must have been mad to come here. You're a maddening, immature little fool. You have a lot of growing up to do before any sane man would want to get involved with you. I knew it was madness to see you again, but...' He broke off, his face grim.

'But?' Marie's heart was racing, her body turning to water as she stared up at his dark, angry face.

He gave a despairing groan. 'If I had any sense I'd walk out of that door without another word!'

'Then why don't you?' She turned away, her movement bringing her hair flicking across his cheek in a scented swathe.

'God help me, I can't,' Stonor murmured under his breath.

Marie felt a suffocating excitement as he reached a hand up to touch her averted face, turning it back to face him, his fingers moving against her skin with the sensitivity of a blind man trying to see with his finger tips.

Slowly he traced the shape of her features; the slender straight nose with its faint upturning, the modelling of her cheekbones, the curved pink mouth. Everywhere his fingers rested she felt fiery nerves spring up, beating in response.

He stared down into her wide, very blue eyes, with their flickering lashes constantly hiding the expression the eyes held.

'Can you imagine what it feels like to be split in half?' he asked her suddenly. 'One part of me has always longed for the emptiness of the desert, the silence, the space. The other half is drawn to the neon lights and crowds of the cities. All my life I've had to fight down the impulse to leave the modern world, and all that it means, behind me; to spend my days out there in the freedom of the desert. I waste much of my energy fighting myself.'

'Why fight it?' she shrugged. 'Why not go there and give up everything else? You're a very rich man. You don't need to pursue even more wealth.'

He smiled sardonically. 'Why don't I go? Because I'm still a young man and I know that to retreat into the ancient, unchanged world of the desert would be cowardice. There's no challenge in the desert that I can't face, but the challenge of the business world does scare me. Every day I hang on an abyss edge. One false move and I go down, everything with me.' His eyes flashed excitedly. 'That's why I stay.'

Marie understood that. She watched his face, darkly alive and glittering, and knew far more about him than she had before. This was a man who loved a hand-to-hand struggle with destiny, with danger. He liked to risk everything on one throw of the dice, loved the thrill of the danger.

'You're mad,' she said softly. 'You can't go on playing Russian roulette with life for ever.'

He grinned down at her, his eyes leaping. 'Can't I? Doesn't that attract you, too, Marie?'

Her breath caught as she met his eyes.

'That night I heard you talking outside the hotel, part of me leapt in wild excitement,' he said quickly. 'You said things I've often thought myself, things I was feeling right then. I, too, was hankering for the desert. I was sick of luxury hotels and silly, flattering fools who think

that money makes a man. I suddenly wanted to play a
game, a game of make-believe; live out the role of my
life, make you believe it too. I took you out into the
desert to fulfil two secret dreams—yours and mine.'

She was breathless, spellbound, as she listened, feeling
the hard-muscled strength of his body against the length
of hers, his arm holding her captive.

Then his face hardened. 'But the reality of it scared
you, didn't it? You're too shallow to meet the challenge
of that vast emptiness, too immature to match a man kiss
for kiss, hunger for hunger...' His voice was stifled by
strong emotion, fires leapt in the dark eyes, there was a
sudden terrifying urgency in the strong hands that held
her, moving over body and face, touching, caressing.

'You're hurting me,' she protested, beginning to
tremble. What had she unleashed? Now, even more than
on that night in the desert, she felt a primitive force in
him which, once let loose, might sweep away everything
that stood in its path.

'I want to hurt you,' he said fiercely. 'I want to sting
you to life. You're like an android, an artificial creation
shaped like a woman, with all a woman's beauty and
desirability, but lacking the vital spark which lights it up.
I told myself that it was folly to come here. It isn't in you
to respond to any man.'

'Then why don't you go?' she blazed, flushed with
pain and anger at what he had said.

He swore under his breath. The hawk-like face was so
close she could see every detail in sharp clarity; the dark,
mysterious eyes so deep looking into them was like falling down a well, the strong nose and fleshless cheekbones, austerely planed, the cruel mouth which was sud-

denly moving closer and closer ...

'No!' she moaned, suffocating under that ruthless pressure, her hands beating at his chest like white moths against a window.

The world swung in a crazy arc around her, fire sprang up wherever his hands touched her. Her heart beat so fast she thought she must faint, as if her senses were not capable of meeting the demands he made upon them. Stonor ignored her struggles, her stifled protests. Compelling, ruthless, merciless, he kissed her until she was clinging weakly to him as to a rock in the midst of a flooding river, half drowning, half ecstatic.

Behind her closed lids a dazzle of light hypnotised her. She clung to him while he kissed her throat, her ears, pushing aside her blouse to kiss her shoulders and the white softness where her breasts rose, panting, from their confinement.

Abruptly he pushed her away so that she stumbled and fell back against the sofa. Opening her eyes, she stared at him, her hair straying in golden wildness across the cushions, her blouse half unbuttoned, her eyes wide and dazed.

For a moment he stared at her, his face grim. Then he bowed sardonically. 'Goodbye, Miss Brinton. It was an education to meet you. I pity the man who's fool enough to fall in love with you. His will be a frustrating experience, trying to spark a flame from the stony emptiness of your heart.'

Turning on his heel, he slammed out of the room, and Marie burst into scalding tears.

# CHAPTER FIVE

SOME weeks later Marie sat on an elaborately worked wicker chair watching a small boy in a white shirt and blue trousers frowning over the drawing he had made of an elephant.

'Should it have five legs?' she asked him lightly. 'Can you remember?'

Jeremy's brown eyes lifted abstractedly. 'It's blue,' he said. 'I haven't got any grey.'

'What about its legs?' she pressed.

He slowly counted them. 'That isn't a leg,' he told her scornfully. 'It's a tail.'

'Oh, sorry.' She got up and bent over the picture. 'It's very good,' she admitted. 'We must try to find some grey pencils next time we go to the market.'

His small face lit up. 'Can we go today? I like going down to the market. I like the candy man. I like that stuff he sells that's pink and sticky. It makes my teeth stick together.'

'Yes,' she said thoughtfully. 'But I'm not sure it's good for your teeth.'

'I like the man who sells crocodile eggs,' Jeremy went on ecstatically. 'What do you think people do with them?'

'I hate to think,' Marie murmured. 'It's nearly time for your lunch.'

'Not rice again,' he moaned. 'I wish I could have chips.'

'You know they don't have potatoes here,' she pointed out.

'I can wish, can't I?' His face was rebellious, the pink skin flushed, the brown eyes cross. 'I'm not very hungry, anyway.'

The heat was enervating for him, Marie thought. She always insisted that he took a nap in the afternoon, when the heat was at its worst, but Jeremy found it hard to sleep in the daytime and often got up again and played with his toys while she was not watching him.

She had made his acquaintance in England, before they left for Jedhpur, and they had become friends at once. Jeremy was a very friendly little boy, quite accustomed to amusing himself, and always delighted to have company. On the long flight from England there had been no difficulty in keeping him amused. He sat drawing huge pictures of fluffy white clouds while he stared out of the window. Marie had been filled with trepidation that day, wondering if she had done the right thing, wondering if she would miss her parents while she was in India, wondering if she would ever be able to manage to look after the little boy.

They had driven from the tiny airstrip into the crowded capital of Jedhpur through narrow streets filled with people who had turned to stare at the black palace car. Few people in Lhalli had cars. They were still an exciting event and attracted a great deal of excited attention. Jeremy had waved, mistakenly imagining all the interest to be in him, and the dark-eyed, white-clad people had sometimes waved back, amused by his smiling little face and bright eyes.

The car had taken them to the pink-washed palace first

of all, driving through a large iron-bolted door held open by two turbanned sentries who saluted, to Jeremy's huge delight.

The palace was sheltered behind great walls behind which lay first the outer courtyard, filled, surprisingly, with goats and boys, who stared and gesticulated as the new arrivals left the car.

'Is it a school?' Jeremy had asked, baffled but enchanted by the goats, with their belled necks and short horns.

'I expect those goats belong to the King,' his mother had said, shrugging.

They had been met at the arched door of the palace by a fierce, turbanned man in spotless white, his broad silk sash fringed where it fell along one hip. He had bowed, hands laid palm to palm, making a courteous greeting. Then he had led them through a bewildering series of marble-floored corridors, their feet echoing as they walked in their Western shoes.

Everywhere they saw sentries and servants, the latter all clad in the same spotless white as the man who was guiding them.

They had waited in a small antechamber for ten minutes before the King arrived, wearing a blue tunic made of some glittering material, buttoned to the throat and falling to his hips, beneath which were white trousers. He had come in suddenly, smiling at them with friendly dark eyes.

'Mrs Cunningham ... how delightful to see you! I hope you had a good flight? And this is your son.' Solemnly he extended a hand to Jeremy, who took it as solemnly.

'I am very glad to meet you,' the King said politely.

Jeremy looked pleased. 'Why are there goats in your courtyard?' he asked eagerly.

The King's round dark eyes smiled. 'Ah, that is because they have come in to be milked,' he said. 'Then they will go back into the fields, up the hills where the grass is green.'

'There were boys too,' Jeremy pointed out.

'They look after the goats,' the King explained. 'Each has his own flock and his own pasture.'

'Why do they wear bells round their necks?' Jeremy asked with an air of scholarly interest.

'So that they can be heard if they get lost,' said the King with great patience.

'Why ...' Jeremy began, but his mother cut him off gently, 'That's enough, Jeremy.'

The King smiled at her. 'He asks intelligent questions.' The dark eyes moved on to scrutinise Marie. 'And this is Miss Brinton, your governess?'

Marie shook hands with him, impressed by his direct and interested manner. He was not at all what she had expected.

'Have you been to this part of the world before?' he asked her. 'What do you think of our small country?'

'I've never been to India before,' she admitted. 'But I'm sure I'm going to like it.'

'This is not India, Miss Brinton,' he said flatly. 'Jedhpur is an independent kingdom with its own history, language and traditions. We are very proud of our past and very hopeful about our future.'

She was embarrassed by her slip, glancing at Jess apologetically, hoping she had not offended the King too much. Jess smiled at her comfortingly, giving a slight shake of the head.

The King clapped his hands and the proud-faced servant in white appeared, bowing profoundly.

'Rahaib, take Miss Brinton and Master Jeremy to their bungalow, will you?' He smiled at Marie. 'I wish to have a long talk with Mrs Cunningham about her work. I hope you will excuse us for a while. Rahaib will see that you have everything you need. If you have any worries, please mention them to him and they will be attended to at once.'

Marie was taken aback, but smiled back politely and allowed Rahaib to lead her and Jeremy away.

Back they went along the marble corridors, her eyes dazedly admiring the gilt glitter of some of the mosaics, staring in fascinated confusion at huge barbaric statues of gods or men, the limbs entwined in strange contortions, the faces calm and impassive. Rahaib walked at a calm pace just ahead of them, one hand loosely hovering around his sash. When someone suddenly slipped out of an alcove between two pale pink pillars Rahaib's hand moved like a snake, flying away from his sash with a curved, glittering dagger between the brown fingers.

'Put that away, Rahaib,' commanded an amused voice.

Rahaib relaxed, bowing. 'Lord, I did not see it was you.'

The newcomer was a young man in Western clothes; a white shirt and loose white trousers, wearing white sports shoes on his feet.

Marie looked at him in curious surprise. He grinned at her, his thin brown face full of mischief.

'I've been playing cricket,' he explained, pointing to

his clothes. 'You must be Mrs Cunningham. I must say, you look amazingly young to be a famous artist.'

She laughed, her blue eyes dancing. 'That's because I'm not Mrs Cunningham. I'm only her son's governess.'

'Ah, yes, the son,' he murmured, glancing at Jeremy, who was a few feet away, inspecting a wall carving of an elephant with much fascination. 'I had forgotten him.' He turned back to her, smiling. 'I am the King's cousin, by the way. My name is Aziz. May I ask your name?'

'Marie Brinton,' she told him.

His voice dropped confidentially. 'I am delighted to meet you, Miss Brinton. You are the answer to a maiden's prayer.'

Her eyebrows curved in silent amusement. She thought he had misunderstood the phrase, but, seeing her unspoken reaction, he grinned at her.

'I mean that literally,' he said. 'I do not suppose the King mentioned Aissa?'

She shook her head. 'Who is Aissa?'

'His sister,' Aziz said softly. 'She has just returned from a year in Paris and she is already beginning to be very bored here. Like myself, she had had a Western education, but now that we are back in Jedhpur we are expected to return to the old ways because otherwise we might shock the people. It is not so bad for me—men have always had more freedom than women here, but for Aissa it is stifling.'

Marie stared at him, uneasy and perplexed. She sensed that she was about to be involved in trouble, but there was little she could do to dodge out of the situation.

Aziz went on pleadingly, 'Aissa badly needs a friend. There are many things she could do with another girl around that she could not do if she were alone. It would not be permitted for her to drive around alone outside the palace, for instance, but if you were her companion her brother would not object.'

'The King seemed very modern-minded,' Marie protested.

Aziz sighed. 'He is, actually, but he can only go so far for fear of offending the diehards who help him run this country. Believe me, plenty of people would make trouble if Aissa was thought to be running wild. She isn't married yet, although she is twenty years old, and to some old-fashioned people that in itself is shocking.'

Marie looked at him in disbelief. 'Shocking?'

'They think she is getting old,' Aziz said grimly. 'A hundred years ago she would have been married at fifteen. The King has held them off until now, but some of them are insisting that he find her a husband without further delay.'

'An arranged marriage?' Marie knew that that was the custom here, so this did not surprise her.

Aziz nodded. 'The Prime Minister is the leader of the old party, the ones who are most determined to have her married off ...'

She glanced nervously at Rahaib, who stood within earshot, his face blank, yet who must have heard every word of this. Aziz followed her glance and smiled.

'Oh, don't worry about Rahaib. He was the King's bodyguard when the King was small. He would die rather than betray any of us.'

Rahaib made no move, no sign indicating that he had heard a word of this remark. Aziz smiled at her again, shrugging.

'You see? He is the eyes and ears, but he does not speak, unless the King commands it.'

'Then the King approves of what you suggest?' she asked doubtfully.

Aziz said softly, 'The King wants his sister to be happy, but he cannot move in the matter himself. He can only permit what she wishes out of his love for her. If she asks to be allowed to visit you in your bungalow, he will agree.'

Rahaib turned suddenly and murmured softly, 'The Lord Hathni approaches, my lord.'

'Oh, gracious heavens,' Aziz said in alarm. He gave Marie a quick look. 'Do not mention that you have seen me. We have never met before.'

Marie was puzzled and alarmed, turning to look down the corridor as she heard the slap of sandalled feet. When she turned back to Aziz he had vanished. She looked at Rahaib in bewilderment. His dark eyes met hers impassively.

Then they moved on slowly, Jeremy still staring at the walls with deep interest. He looked up at Marie, wide-eyed. 'Funny drawings,' he said to her. 'Some of those snakes are all tangled up. Are they fighting?'

'I expect so,' she said, nervously wondering about the approaching footsteps.

The man coming down the corridor was short, rather slightly built and grey-haired, his richly decorated tunic ablaze with colour, his austere face at variance with what he wore. Behind him marched two men in white turbans and red tunics, their faces wearing the same blank impassivity as Rahaib.

He paused as he came face to face with Marie, his

almond-shaped eyes narrowing. Then he smiled politely, without warmth.

Rahaib spoke in the soft local dialect, and the new-comer listened without looking at him.

Then he looked back at Marie and made the usual courteous greeting, hands together, head bowed. 'Miss Brinton! I am Hathni Kundor, the King's chief minister. Welcome to Jedhpur. I hope you had a pleasant journey here.'

'Yes, thank you,' said Marie, slightly nervous in his presence. He had an intimidating eye, cold and clear-sighted, and a soft precision of speech which made every syllable he uttered very formal.

He nodded in response to her reply, glanced briefly at Jeremy and then said politely, 'I hope we shall meet again, Miss Brinton.'

She stood aside, realising he meant to walk on, and with another courteous gesture he and his escort proceeded along the corridor. She let out a long sigh of relief.

'Whew!'

Glancing at Rahaib, she fancied she caught a flicker of something that might have been amusement passing across his face, but the next second he had assumed his usual calm mask.

They made their way out of the palace without further incident, got back into the black limousine and drove out of the palace gates into the teeming city. Soon they were driving between tiny, white-washed flat-roofed houses threaded with alleys which wound away out of sight. Thin, stark-ribbed dogs scratched in the dust. Women in bright silks and soft slippers, their heads draped against the intruding sun, moved from shop to shop with graceful steps. Around an ancient, stone-walled well sat older women, their faces wrinkled and dried up by the sun, gossiping with the ease of old friends, while children in cotton shirts scampered barefoot around them, chasing each other in some ritualistic game.

The streets grew more and more crowded, and the car had trouble inching its way through them. Street-sellers carrying trays of food shouted their wares. A water carrier waddled along, slopping precious drops on either side of his yoked shoulders, followed by a crowd of thirsty dogs who licked at the wet dust.

From street cafés came the high wail of traditional music. A dancing girl in gold-trimmed skirts and bare feet, her ankles and wrists jangling with golden bangles, came out of a café to stare at them as they drove past.

Marie was delighted by one shop, the flat stall in front of it swathed in rainbow-coloured silks, red, yellow, green, blue, flung across the stall in voluminous folds to catch the eye, the gold and silver threads woven into the material glittering in the sunlight. The shopkeeper, seeing her eager eyes, bowed invitingly, but the car drove on slowly.

Jeremy only really grew interested when the car temporarily halted, to let a flock of goats pass, outside a sweet stall. Wooden bowls full of sticky pink and white sweets drew the attentions of a horde of black flies, at which the perspiring stallholder slapped with a paper fan. Across the street stood a cookshop from which the odour of spicy curry floated. Outside stood a boy not much older than Jeremy, hawking a woven basket of palm leaves; stuffed with cardamon-scented rice and minced mutton,

Rahaib informed them. A smile briefly lit his count-
enance as he added, 'Most delicious, my lady.'

'Can I buy some?' Jeremy asked eagerly.

Marie smiled at him. 'Another day, perhaps.' She was
not altogether certain of the safety of eating food from
the market. The flies which pervaded the place worried
her. None of the food seemed to be covered from the sun;
even the meat lay uncovered, descended upon by black
tides of flies.

They moved on jerkily, the driver apparently unflur-
ried or annoyed by the constant stops necessitated by the
throngs of people who poured past his bonnet. Soon
Jeremy saw something else he liked: a stall selling toys;
little wooden birds which pecked at painted corn on a
bright green board when you pulled the string below,
elephants of bright blue which had nodding heads, pea-
cocks with vivid bejewelled tails that opened and closed
like fans, little wooden men who swung over and over a
string stretched between two poles, windmills of painted
paper which whirled round and round when you blew
them.

'When can we come here again?' Jeremy asked her
eagerly.

'We'll ask your mother,' she promised.

'Soon? Tomorrow?'

'Perhaps,' she said, not liking to commit herself yet.
She must see what Mrs Cunningham thought about the
market before she agreed to take Jeremy there.

Rahaib said quietly, 'I will escort you and the child to
the market whenever you wish, Miss Brinton.'

She looked at him gratefully. 'Thank you, Rahaib.
That's very kind of you.'

He shook his head. 'The King's highness has told me to see that you and the child come to no harm. While you are in Jedhpur I am your servant, miss.'

'Oh. I see.' She was taken aback, wondering how she was going to cope with his constant presence day after day.

He smiled then, his face gravely amused. 'When you need me I shall be in the servants' quarters of the bungalow, my lady.'

She flushed, seeing that he had read her mind. 'Thank you, Rahaib,' she said in faint apology.

He inclined his head. 'It is my pleasure,' he said formally. 'There are certain persons in Jedhpur who do not approve of the King's royal desire to modernise the kingdom. They resent foreigners, and they might make trouble for you if you went out alone. That is why the King's highness has asked me to guard you.'

She looked at him anxiously. 'You mean it's dangerous for us to go out without you?'

'It would be wiser not to do so,' he agreed. 'Most of our people are gentle and hospitable, but there are some who hate the new ways and wish only for things to go on as they have always done ... these people are trouble-makers.'

She remembered what Aziz had said. 'And the Prime Minister himself does not approve, I gather?' she asked.

Rahaib's face stiffened. 'My Lord Hathni prefers the old ways,' he agreed politely. He looked at her directly. 'But you need not fear him, my lady. Lord Hathni is a very good man.'

'Aziz seemed afraid of him,' she said, half to herself.

Rahaib hesitated, then said gently, 'My lord Aziz respects his father too much to fear him, my lady.'

She stared at him in astonishment. 'His father?'

Rahaib inclined his head. 'Lord Hathni is the King's highness's uncle.'

'And Aziz is his son,' she said. 'Then why did he hide?'

'Because he did not wish his father to see him speaking with you,' Rahaib explained. 'Lord Hathni might then have suspected when you saw much of the Princess Aissa that it was his son's doing...'

'I see,' she said, not really seeing very much at all. Clearly, the politics of Jedhpur were involved and dangerous. She wished Aziz had not dragged her into them, and decided that if at all possible she would steer completely clear of anything which even remotely smelt of politics. She did not want to cause trouble here for Jess or for the King.

'Thank you for telling me, Rahaib,' she said, looking at the grizzled old man with gratitude.

'I thought you should know, Miss Brinton,' he said simply. 'Prince Aziz is not always very thoughtful or considerate of other people. He sees only his own desires and seeks a way to achieve them.'

'I suppose it was kind of him to wish to help Princess Aissa, anyway,' she said.

Rahaib's eyes met hers briefly. The old man seemed to hesitate, then shrugged, saying nothing. She wondered what it was he had decided not to tell her.

They had left the market quarter behind them now, and were driving along a wide, dusty road fringed with square-built white houses with the usual flat roofs. Wire fences strung from wooden posts surrounded their gardens. Thickly set rhododendron bushes, deodars, fruit trees and dancing flies inhabited these gardens. Their shade was alluring, and Marie stared at each one, hoping it would be theirs.

At last they halted outside one and Rahaib stood to watch them dismount from the car, then unlocked the high gate and escorted them up the dusty path.

There were two doors; one outer with a mesh-wire covering to keep out flies, one inner made all of glass to let light into the house. A long verandah ran the length of the back of the house. Wicker chairs were arranged around a low cane table.

A small, slender woman in a yellow sari came hurrying from somewhere to greet them politely. Over her palms her dark eyes looked curiously at Marie. A red caste mark in the middle of her forehead enhanced the glowing colour of her olive skin.

'Lispa speaks no English,' Rahaib told them. 'I shall interpret for you if you tell me your wishes.'

Marie smiled at Lispa and indicated Jeremy. 'Tell her the little boy is tired and hungry.'

Lispa's dark eyes travelled to Jeremy as Rahaib spoke to her. A little smile touched her mouth. She held out one thin-fingered hand to the boy, who trustingly took her hand and let her lead him away.

Rahaib ushered Marie along a corridor to a shuttered room full of cool shadows. 'This is your chamber, my lady. Your boxes are here already.'

Heaving a sigh of delight at the coolness, she looked around the room, gazing at the net-enshrouded bed, the carved chests and the wicker, cushioned chair. 'It's delightful,' she told Rahaib.

'Will you rest or eat, my lady?'

'I think we'd better eat first,' she said.

He bowed. 'I will go and find out if the food is ready. Please, wash and refresh yourself.'

She looked at him doubtfully, and he smiled at her. 'There is a bathroom beyond that door,' he told her gently.

Marie was astonished. 'A bathroom?' She had not expected such a thing here.

'This house belonged once to an American who came to study our old temples,' Rahaib explained. 'He had a bathroom built into the bungalow. Of course, we have no modern sanitation in most of our houses. The American dug a pit for the waste out at the back of the house and laid pipes to carry the wastage out there. It took many months and by the time he had finished he was just leaving to go home.' A faint look of amusement came into the dark eyes. 'He was not pleased.'

'Your English is very good, Rahaib,' she told him admiringly. 'Have you been to Europe?'

He looked surprised. 'Of course I accompanied the King when he went to school and university in England. I spent fourteen years in your country.'

'Fourteen years?' She was astonished. 'No wonder your English is so good!'

'The King's highness was seven when his royal father sent him to school at first. We stayed there until he had finished his whole education. Every year we came home for the summer, of course. I could have married then, but I waited. Until my lord the King was home for good I would not wed.'

'And are you married now?' she asked curiously.

He looked surprised. 'But Lispa is my wife,' he said.

'Oh, I see,' she said, taken aback, remembering the formal way in which he had addressed Lispa, the commanding note in his voice. He had spoken to her as if to a servant.

'Have you any children, Rahaib?' she asked.

He smiled. 'Three sons.' His pride was evident. 'Lispa is a good wife.'

She was amused. 'Is the King married too?'

Rahaib's eyes glowed suddenly. 'The King is married,' he nodded. 'The Queen expects her first child in two months. We all pray it will be a son.' He hesitated and again she was sure he doubted whether it would be discreet to speak, then he said softly, 'The Queen is most beautiful and sweet. Her voice is like melted honey, her skin like silk.'

Marie looked at him curiously. He sounded as if he worshipped the Queen, she thought. He had not had that gentle, adoring ring in his voice when he spoke of Lispa. Perhaps his love for the King carried over to the King's wife.

'How old is the Queen?' she asked curiously.

'Fifteen,' Rahaib said.

'Fifteen!' Marie was astonished. It seemed very young to be a Queen and expecting a first child, but then she knew that things were very different here. She thought of herself at fifteen, a hockey-playing schoolgirl with white socks and a short gym tunic, and suppressed a smile. Indeed, things were very different.

When Rahaib had left her she went into the bathroom. It was a stark, whitewashed room. The bath was sunk into the floor, which had been concreted, perhaps to discourage insects. When she turned on the taps the water issued in a discouraging brown stream, but after running for a while the water cleared, although occasionally a dead fly fell out with it.

She locked the door and had a brief bath, then dried herself and dressed again. When she returned to her bedroom she found Jeremy there, sitting on her bed, staring around.

'I'm sleepy,' he said fretfully.

'Bed, then,' she said, lifting him down. He was limp and heavy, his eyes glazed with weariness. She carried him through to the tiny room which Rahaib had said was for him, undressed him and popped him into bed. She had barely left the room before his even breathing announced that he was asleep. It had been a long journey, she thought. It was not surprising that he was so tired.

Jess had returned from the palace some hours later, having eaten with the King, her eyes excited as she told Marie about the plans she and the King had laid for the work ahead.

'I'm going to enjoy this,' she said delightedly. 'What about you? Are you settling in?'

Marie had said she was already feeling quite at home here, and Jess had given her an approving look.

Their first day in Jedhpur had ended peacefully as the darkness fell with the swiftness of a hawk, cloaking everything with shadows.

And so their life began to take on a routine. Each day Jess got up at dawn, breakfasted on fruit and warm chapattis, then drove off in a Land-Rover the King had lent her to start sketching in the isolation of her stilt hut in the marshes. While she was gone, Marie amused Jeremy on the verandah of the house.

Drawing elephants and tigers was his favourite occupation. Like his mother, he had a natural talent for it, and a deep curiosity about everything around him.

When he was not with Jess, he liked to play in the kitchen with Lispa's sons, who were close to his age and possessed exciting toys similar to those he had seen in the market. He and Marie had already visited the market with Lispa to help her choose food and to see the fascinating shops at closer quarters. Jeremy had bought some pencils, a wooden elephant with a jewelled head-cloth and bright eyes, and a large plastic ball imported from Europe.

Today as they trailed back into the house for their midday meal Jeremy demanded another visit to the market. Marie promised one tomorrow, with which he was content.

He showed Lispa his drawing of the great blue elephant, and she admired it, clicking her brightly painted fingernails in delight.

Jeremy eyed the food laid out for them with faint depression—a plate of steaming white rice, a bowl of vegetable curry, a pile of warm chapattis and some fruit in a carved wooden bowl.

'Rice again!' he groaned, and Lispa looked at him anxiously.

Marie spoke to her in the local dialect. 'Good, very good.' She had been learning a few phrases from Rahaib in order to be able to speak to Lispa in her own tongue. The young woman's face cleared and she smiled, amicably making her little gesture of polite recognition.

'You mustn't hurt Lispa's feelings, Jeremy,' Marie said gently. 'She works very hard to make your meals. You must try to like them.'

'They're always the same,' he said crossly. 'Curry, curry, curry . . .'

'Last night we had chicken cooked in the oven,' she pointed out.

'It didn't taste like chicken,' said Jeremy. 'It was all hot and spicy.'

Marie sighed. At his age it was difficult to adjust, she supposed. She helped him to a small portion of rice and curry and he poked at it with his fork, his face sulky.

Rahaib appeared behind her chair and bent to say quietly, 'An Englishman to see you, Miss Brinton.'

Suddenly her heart leapt on a wild, ludicrous hope. 'An Englishman? Did he give a name?'

'He is an archaeologist called Davidson,' Rahaib explained. 'He is living here while he studies our temples— many archaeologists come here to study them. They live in a bungalow near them and rarely come into Lhalli.'

'Davidson?' She did not know the name, but she said that Rahaib might show him in, and the old man departed to do so.

'Miss Brinton? I'm so sorry to disturb you during your meal!' The voice was young, cheerful, with the unmistakable burr of a West Country accent running beneath the English.

She smiled, holding out her hand. 'Mr Davidson? Do sit down and join us. There's more than enough for three.'

'Well, thanks,' he said at once, taking a chair. 'I must

admit, I'm hungry. I've been trailing around Lhalli all morning trying to see the King, but they won't admit me to the palace. That's why I'm here, to tell you the truth.'

She was puzzled, staring at him across the table. He was in his late twenties, fair-faced, with wiry brown hair and clear, friendly hazel eyes. She liked him on sight. He had a direct and cheerful manner which was appealing. 'How can I help you?'

'You work for Mrs Cunningham,' he said, accepting a plate from Lispa with a smile. 'And she works for the King. She could get him to see me.'

Marie laughed. 'Oh, I don't know about that. She hasn't seen the King since we arrived. They talked for a while on the first day, but he's been busy ever since.'

'All the same, if she wrote to him I think he might take some notice of her.'

'Why do you want to see him so badly?' she asked.

He forked some curry into his mouth, chewed and swallowed, then looked round at Lispa, who was discreetly hovering within earshot. He spoke in quick dialect for a moment, and Lispa's face beamed at him.

'Mr Davidson, do you speak the local language?' she asked him curiously.

He nodded. 'I've learnt it since I got here.'

'How long have you been here?' she asked.

'Three months.'

'Three months?' She was astounded. 'But ... you sound quite fluent...'

He shrugged modestly. 'I have a flair for languages—I speak eleven. It's just a knack.' Then he grinned at her. 'By the way, my name is Peter.'

She acknowledged the invitation with a smile. 'Mine is

Marie, Peter. So why do you need to see the King?'

He leaned forward. 'I want to see a temple some miles out in the jungle and apparently it's forbidden to go anywhere near it. It's sacred, or something. I'm not sure why there's a taboo on it, but when I tried to drive there the other day I was forbidden to go any further by a very officious village headman, so I want to see the King to ask his permission. He's usually very good about these things—he's a modern-minded chap. But they denied me entrance to the palace, too. Probably old Hathni. He hates the sight of me and makes no bones about it. If I could get a message to the King I'm sure he would give me permission.'

Marie glanced at Rahaib's impassive face. 'Well, I'll speak to Mrs Cunningham, but I can't promise anything.'

Peter Davidson looked at Rahaib, too. 'What do you think, Rahaib?'

'I cannot say, sir,' Rahaib returned blandly.

'Hmm . . .' Peter looked at Marie and grinned. 'That means he refuses to get involved. Discreet chap, Rahaib.'

'You've met him before?'

Peter laughed. 'Anyone who meets the King meets Rahaib. He's the King's shadow.'

'He's our shadow for the moment,' said Marie, smiling at Rahaib. 'He's been very kind to us.'

Peter looked across the table at Jeremy. 'Enjoying your lunch, young chap?'

'No,' said Jeremy sulkily. 'I'm fed up with rice, and with curry and chapattis . . .'

Marie frowned at him. 'Jeremy! That's rude!'

'No,' said Peter cheerfully, 'just honest. I tell you what,

Jeremy—why don't you come to dinner with me tonight and I'll give you real English food?'

Jeremy's face lit up. 'Chips?' he asked eagerly.

'I don't know about chips,' said Peter, scratching his chin. 'I could give you new potatoes and sausages, though.'

'Sausages?' Jeremy's face shone with delight. 'Honestly?' He stared at him as if at Santa Claus. 'And potatoes? Marie said there were no potatoes in Jedhpur!' He glared at her accusingly.

Peter winked at her. 'I've got a secret supply. Will you come?' He looked at Marie appealingly.

'Oh, please,' Jeremy begged.

She smiled. 'I suppose I can hardly refuse. Jeremy would never forgive me.'

'Neither would I,' Peter assured her.

# CHAPTER SIX

WHEN Jess returned from her day out in the marshes she was hot and grimy, her feet plastered with black mud, her shirt sticking to her back after the heat of the day. She paused, to say hallo, before going to the bathroom to take a quick bath. Jeremy giggled at the sight of her.

'You're dirty, Mummy!'

'Filthy,' she agreed cheerfully. Under her arm she carried a bulging portfolio. 'But I've done a lot of work today. I saw a tiger down by the water hole, a splendid brute with enormous muscles, in fine condition. He stayed there for half an hour very obligingly and I was able to make several good sketches of him.'

'Jess, we've had an invitation,' Marie informed her.

Jeremy chimed in excitedly. 'Yes, we're going to have potatoes for supper tonight.'

Jess laughed. 'Potatoes?' Her brows rose. 'That sounds very unlikely, darling.'

'We are, aren't we?' he claimed indignantly, giving Marie a look of appeal.

'Yes,' she agreed. She looked at Jess and smiled. 'A young man called today and invited us all to supper. He offered us potatoes and sausages—Jeremy couldn't believe his ears. I'm afraid I could hardly turn him down once Jeremy had heard that.'

Jess laughed again. 'Who was this conjuror?'

'An English archaeologist,' Marie told her. 'Peter Davidson. He was rather nice.'

'I see,' said Jess with amusement. 'Well, in that case, I suppose you'd better go to your orgy, the pair of you.'

'Oh, you must come too,' Marie urged.

Jess shook her head. 'I'm too tired. I'll send my apologies—I want to go to bed early.'

'Mummy, when can I come and see your house on stilts?' begged Jeremy. 'I want to watch tigers and elephants.'

'Why not tomorrow?' she replied easily. 'You and Marie can both come. But you'll have to be very quiet while I'm working, Jeremy, you know that.'

'Promise!' he breathed ecstatically.

Jess laughed and went on to have her bath while Rahaib drove Marie and Jeremy along the dusty roads to the bungalows near the temple clearing where the English archaeological party were living.

They were passing through wilder country than they had ever seen before. The houses out here were smaller, thatched with dried grass, their mud walls baked hard by the sun. Thin cattle with great bells around their necks roamed the fields. The jungle was never far away, gloomy with shade, hung with creepers which festooned the struggling trees like Christmas chains. Jungle fowl with red combs and orange necks flew up squawking as they drove past, then settled again to scratch in the leafy dust. Strange red flowers made patches of brightness in the green of the jungle. Among the leafy branches sat parakeets of many colours, mocking them raucously, their round bright eyes following the car out of sight.

'It's rather creepy in there, isn't it?' Jeremy whispered, his small fingers clutching at Marie's hand.

'I'm afraid it is,' she agreed gently. 'But we would be

quite safe with Rahaib to protect us.'

Rahaib turned his huge head to grin at Jeremy, his teeth white except for several sheathed in glittering gold. His fierce moustaches bristled proudly. 'I have shot many tigers,' he told Jeremy. 'No need to be afraid while I am there.'

Jeremy looked at him thoughtfully. 'You're very strong, aren't you, Rahaib?'

Rahaib laughed. 'Very strong,' he agreed.

They came to a clearing in the jungle where the ornately carved cupolas of temples reared like mirages against the encroaching green gloom. Nearby stood a wire fence surrounding several roughly constructed bungalows. On the verandah of one stood Peter Davidson, a glass in his hand as he waved to them.

Rahaib followed them on to the verandah and stood impassively while Peter greeted them, then, when they were led into the house, sat down on the steps of the verandah and stared out into the swiftly falling dusk.

'My friends wanted to get in on the act,' Peter said cheerfully, pouring Jeremy a glass of lemonade and a glass of lime laced slightly with gin for Marie, 'but I told them to clear off. This is my party, I said. Find your own visitors.' He glanced at the darkening windows. 'I expect they're watching us sulkily right now.'

'Oh, what a shame,' said Marie, almost laughing. 'How many of you are there?'

'Four of us,' he told her. 'Our leader is Grant Williams, a choleric Welshman of advancing years. Then there's Duffy, who's Irish and addicted to poker, Saintsbury, who's of rather monkish habits, never drinking or having any fun—and me.' He grinned at her. 'I'm the pick of the bunch, believe me. I didn't want you to meet the others yet in case they frightened you off. En masse they can be pretty horrifying.'

Jeremy was gazing around the room with a disillusioned air. 'I don't see any potatoes and sausages,' he said.

Marie gave Peter a warning glance. 'I hope for your sake that you weren't just having him on, because he's set his heart on those potatoes of yours.'

He bowed. 'When I promise something I mean every word I say.' He picked up a brass bell and rang it with abandon. A few moments later an old man in a turban and dhoti came into the room bearing a large brass tray. While Jeremy watched with glee he laid the table with three plates, lit the candles and then placed some covered dishes in the centre.

'Right-ho, Ramji,' said Peter cheerfully. 'We'll do the rest.' He waved them to their seats, then whipped the covers away. Jeremy gave a sigh of rapture. Nestling in one was a pile of small new potatoes shining with butter, faintly dusted with what appeared to be chopped chives. In the other was a mound of sausages swimming in baked beans.

'How did you do it?' Marie demanded as Peter piled the food on to Jeremy's eager plate.

'Tins,' he said succinctly.

She burst out laughing, then her eyes brightened. 'Where did you get them?' If Peter could buy tins of English food, she thought, so could they.

Peter shook his head. 'Brought them from England,' he admitted. 'They were shipped out with our heavy equipment, strictly for special occasions. We could only bring a small supply or I'd give you some.'

She sighed. 'Oh, well, it's wonderful to have a change, as Jeremy says.'

'You might be able to get them from one of the larger towns,' he suggested. 'Of course, there's no demand for such stuff in Lhalli, but in Delhi or Calcutta there's an English population who have such food imported for them.'

'It doesn't matter,' she said, enjoying the buttery taste of the potatoes.

They had fruit and custard to follow, the custard also coming from a tin, Peter informed her. Then they had coffee, strong and milky. Afterwards while Jeremy looked through some coloured books of photographs of India which Peter produced, Marie and Peter played records and talked by candlelight.

Suddenly their peace was interrupted by the tramp of feet on the verandah. Peter looked round, grimacing.

'Blast them! I might have known they wouldn't keep out...'

Then three men came into the room, eagerly looking at Marie. Peter sulkily introduced her to them. They surrounded her, talking all at once, making her laugh.

'I've discovered why you aren't allowed out near the Satmu temple,' Grant Williams, a short dark man in his thirties, said to Peter.

'Oh?' Peter asked impatiently.

'Apparently Mrs Cunningham is behind it,' said Grant, smiling at Marie.

'Jess?' Marie was puzzled.

He turned to her, his dark eyes twinkling. 'It seems she doesn't want any visitors out there for the moment in case they scare away any of the animals who visit the waterhole. The temple is just a few hundred yards away in the jungle.'

'So that's it!' Peter exploded. 'Well, it seems simple then. All I have to do is get her to take me out there with her.'

'We're going there tomorrow,' Marie told him.

Peter's face lit up. 'That's terrific! I'll come, too.'

'Oh, I don't know,' she protested. 'You'd have to ask Jess.'

'I'll come back and ask her tonight,' Peter said.

'How are you going to get back?' Grant asked him sarcastically. 'I need the Land-Rover to get into Lhalli to send some telegrams.'

'You can give me a lift back,' Peter said confidently.

Grant shook his head. 'I have a better idea. Strange as it may seem, I'm still in charge of this expedition. I'll see Mrs Cunningham for you and ask her permission for a visit to the temple.'

Peter looked at him unwillingly, and Grant grinned. 'Don't argue, old man. You can't descend on Mrs Cunningham at this hour and foist yourself on her until I get back from Lhalli. You know how long it takes to send a telegram here.'

So they drove back to the bungalow with Grant Williams driving behind them, and he came into the bungalow to have a few words with Jess.

She was startled to see him. Wrapped in a cotton dressing-gown, her short hair hair damp from her bath, she flushed as she shook hands.

'I'm sorry to intrude at this hour,' he said uneasily, and explained his mission.

'If Mr Davidson comes along tomorrow he must be

very quiet,' Jess said. 'I don't want any disturbances near the waterhole. The animals scent any intruders and keep clear for hours until they're sure the coast is clear.'

'I'll bring him myself,' said Grant. 'I think I can vouch for his discretion if I'm there beside him.'

Jess lifted amused blue eyes to him. 'I see,' she said, her glance measuring him.

'Will you trust me?' he asked.

'I think I will,' she said softly.

Next morning at dawn they all set off in two Land-Rovers. Jess, Marie and Jeremy drove in one, Peter, Grant Williams and Rahaib came behind them in another. The journey was slow and painful. The roads were soon nothing but cart-tracks through the jungle, jolting roughly over them they clenched their teeth at each great bump, their faces soon grey with dust.

Soon they left the Land-Rovers parked in a clearing and went the rest of the way on foot, walking carefully in single file through dark jungle paths, listening to the screech of green parakeets overhead, watching the flicker of wings as greenshanks and golden orioles flew between the branches.

'We shall be coming to the river soon,' Jess said softly.

The heat was oppressive, steamy, humid. High grass whispered on all sides of them under the shade of the twisted creepers. At dawn the mist was still slowly clearing from the river banks; a luminous pearly whiteness hung around them everywhere.

Suddenly a kingfisher flew out, a silver fish in its beak, the flash of bright blue making them jump.

'Here we are,' Jess whispered.

They emerged on a river bank, the sides stony with pebbles. A few feet away on the other side some roe deer, small spotted deer with liquid eyes, were grazing. They shot away, vanishing into the mist with a silent speed that was very impressive.

Jeremy froze, clutching his mother's arm. She followed the stare of his round eyes and smiled.

'It won't hurt you, darling. It's only a monitor.'

The lizard slowly moved into the safety of the jungle again, his green skin merging with the trees.

They moved on towards the stilt hut the King had had built for Jess. Thatched with dry grass, open-sided, it was reached by a rickety series of bamboo steps, like a ladder. Below the stilts it stood on the grass was trodden flat and yellowing.

'Doesn't look too safe to me,' Grant Williams observed with a frown.

Jess laughed. 'It does very well for me.' Then she surveyed them all with a little grimace. 'But you may be right. I doubt if it would support the weight of a small army like you. Some of you must stay below for a while.'

'I'll take Marie off to see the temple,' Peter said eagerly.

'I'll stay with you, Mummy,' Jeremy insisted, clinging to her hand.

She looked at Rahaib, who inclined his head politely. 'If you will permit, my lady, I will visit the village and see if I can find fresh milk and eggs.'

'That would be nice,' Jess thanked him. 'You know where it is, Rahaib?'

A look of dry amusement crossed his face. 'Yes, my lady.'

Grant Williams laughed. 'Rahaib knows where everything is,' he told Jess.

Peter took Marie's hand. 'Coming? The temple must be along here somewhere . . .'

'No, sir,' Rahaib interrupted. 'It is along that path over there . . .' His brown finger pointed confidently to a very narrow, overgrown path.

'Thanks,' said Peter, with a grin. He and Marie took the path indicated, finding it heavy going because it was so overgrown. Peter slashed at the creepers with a sinister-looking knife he had carried with him from the Land-Rover. The river ran to the right of them, chuckling over great grey boulders.

They came out in another clearing, facing the temple, which was in a far more ruinous state than the ones Peter and his colleagues were working on, its steps crumbling away, the jungle growing in upon it closer and closer, creepers strangling the ornate pillars which decorated it, grass growing through the stone flags of the courtyard.

'What a mess!' Peter said reflectively.

'How old is it?' she asked him, staring at it with great interest and fascination.

'Looks older than the ones we're working on,' Peter shrugged. 'Perhaps third century.'

'As old as that?' she demanded.

He laughed. 'India is a very ancient country. Let's take a look inside.'

They walked up the steps and entered the temple. The sunlight died as they went inside and cool shadows thickened the air. The smell was nauseating.

'Something rather dead in here,' Peter said, grimacing. 'An animal has got in and died, presumably.'

'I'll wait for you by the door,' said Marie, feeling sickened by the smell.

Peter glanced at her. 'Are you all right?'

'Fine,' she said. 'I just prefer the open air.'

He laughed. 'I know what you mean. Look, I won't be long, then I'll guide you back to the others.'

'There's no hurry,' she said. 'It's quite pleasant here.'

Peter plunged further into the gloom, leaving her by the door, staring into the oppressive jungle. She saw a giant spider's web glistening with silvery mist drops stretched across from one pillar to the other. The carvings were so unfamiliar, so contorted and strange, that her eyes wearied of tracing them, trying to make sense of them. She knew nothing of the ancient legends that lay behind them, the mysteries and secrets of the religion that had caused this place to be built.

Suddenly she froze, her whole body shaken with horror. Facing her, between the creeper-straggled trees, stood a huge tiger, sleek, muscled, poised for movement, his tail lashing from side to side, the green eyes staring at her unwinkingly.

She was so frightened that she merely stared back, swallowing on a terror so great she felt sick.

She opened her mouth to scream for Peter, but no sound came. She felt her limbs turn to water.

The tiger's head slowly drew forward. She saw the great body tense for a spring, every muscle beneath his shining coat.

She remembered Jess describing a tiger who had visited the waterhole beneath the stilt house. This must be the same one. Jess had said he left pug marks so big that she had measured them with disbelief.

A sudden crash among the trees drew her attention from him. The tiger too turned to stare, distracted from her.

Someone was moving among the trees, and Marie realised that the newcomer might walk straight into the tiger. She screamed then, her throat relaxed from the grip of terror.

'Tiger! Don't come any further ... there's a tiger here...' The words seemed to float mistily on the morning air. For a wild moment she wondered if she had actually said them, then she heard Peter racing towards her from the back of the temple, his feet stumbling on the stone floors. At the same time the unknown person began to run through the jungle, but incredibly towards her, not away into safety.

The creeper-hung trees swayed noisily, then a figure emerged, just a few feet from the tiger's crouched body. With incredulous dismay Marie recognised the tall, dark man in white shirt and casual beige slacks, his head cocked as he took in the scene confronting him.

The tiger flicked his tail with a lazy motion, turning his head to survey the new arrival on the scene, and Peter panted up beside Marie, flinging a protective arm around her.

'What's up?' he demanded. 'I heard you scream...' Then his eyes flashed down into the little clearing and he swore under his breath.

'God!' He fumbled at his belt and gave a groan of dismay. 'My pistol! I left it in the temple...'

As he turned to go and get it, she said quickly, 'I'll go. Try to distract the tiger. Keep it occupied. Make a lot of noise—try to frighten it away.'

She ran into the darkness, searching the gloom with eyes that at first could take nothing in, then she saw the scuffed trail of Peter's footsteps across the centuries of leaf mould which had fallen down through the open arches in the walls and made a carpet across part of the floor. She ran forward, following the trail of Peter's feet, until she came to a fallen block of masonry on which lay an open notebook, some pencils and the pistol. Light reflected back from the metal of the pistol as she picked it up and turned to run back.

She heard Peter shouting, stamping his feet. The tiger made a deep menacing sound in his throat, then gave an appalling roar of rage.

Peter shouted again, in alarm. 'Run ... get back!'

Terror chilled Marie's blood. It seemed an eternity until she could reach the door, and her eyes, accustomed now to the gloom inside, had to adjust to the dazzle of sunlight before she could take in what was happening.

Stonor was on his back, wrestling helplessly with the huge animal, while Peter was gallantly slashing at its eyes with a bamboo stake. She saw wet stains of sweat spread across the back of his shirt.

She had once been shown how to fire a pistol. Instinct made her now fling up her arm, her eyes narrowing on the tiger's head. The recoil of the shot made her deaf for a moment, then she was able to hear and see again.

The tiger had vanished. Her shot had missed, somehow, but it had frightened the beast away. The leaves swayed in the jungle, testifying to his departure. She ran down the steps and flung herself down beside Stonor. He was clasping one shoulder, a red stain spreading from beneath his fingers.

'Let me see . . .' she said anxiously.

'No!' His voice bit out curtly. 'Leave it alone!'

She felt hot colour run up under her skin, and drew back. Peter looked at her sympathetically. He lifted her, a hand under her elbow, and put an arm around her waist.

'Look,' he said gently, 'that tiger may come back. I can't go and leave you two alone here, and I can't let you run back to the others alone, so we'll have to help this fellow back there together. If he isn't hurt badly he may be able to walk with our help.'

Stonor ground out harshly, 'Lift me. I can walk without help once I'm on my feet.'

Peter gently helped him to his feet. Stonor swayed, still holding his torn shoulder. There was blood running down his arm and along the side of his ripped shirt now.

'Here, take my arm,' said Peter.

Stonor drew back, frowning. 'I'm all right.' He began to walk steadily, with that upright loping pace which was so characteristic of him, and Peter, giving her a wry grimace, followed him. Marie came after them more slowly, her mind in confusion.

What was Stonor doing here? Had he been looking for her? She looked at his straight, graceful back, the dark hair ruffled by the fight, the broad powerful shoulders held tensely in pain. Of course he must have been here looking for her. Hadn't she known, all the time, inwardly that he would come? When Peter arrived suddenly unannounced, hadn't she thought it was Stonor? She had known that sooner or later Stonor would turn up.

'What on earth were you doing strolling through the jungle in that lighthearted fashion, anyway?' Peter was asking him. 'I was staggered when I saw you. Where did you spring from?'

'Lhalli,' Stonor said grimly.

'What's your name? I'm Peter Davidson, by the way. I'm with the British archaeological expedition in Jedhpur.' He looked back at Marie. 'This is Miss . . .'

'I know,' Stonor interrupted in that curt fashion. Was he in much pain? Marie wondered anxiously.

Peter looked from one to the other of them, his brows raised. 'Oh, you know each other.'

'My name is Grey,' Stonor told him.

'Friend of Miss Brinton?'

'We've met,' said Stonor.

Peter was baffled, glancing back enquiringly at her, as if to ask her what he was to make of this laconic, tight-lipped stranger. But she glanced away without revealing anything.

'Are you an artist like Mrs Cunningham?' Peter asked, struck by a sudden thought.

'No.'

Peter glanced back at Marie again, then shrugged, seeing that he would get no help from her in his interrogation. They came out beside the river. At their abrupt arrival a gaggle of white egrets made a hawking sound of rage and vanished from their fishing in the shallows of the waterpool below the stilt hut. A peacock stalking on the far bank rattled with irritation at them. Far along the river bank came the loud splash as a mugger slid down the mud into the water, his wicked little eyes blinking above his long snout. As if it had been some sort of signal the other muggers basking on the bank in the sun, for all the world like a row of grey-brown logs, came to life and slid down after him, making a series of splashes which awoke the monkeys in the tree tops and sent them chattering and swinging across the jungle.

From the stilt hut they saw faces peering crossly at them. Then heard an exclamation of alarm. Soon Jess, Grant Williams and Jeremy had descended to them to investigate, having seen the blood on Stonor's shirt.

A few moments later Rahaib came swinging through the jungle at an easy pace carrying a woven basket of eggs and some goat's milk in a wide-lipped jug.

Calmly, despite Stonor's displeasure, he made him take away his hand from the mauled shoulder, frowning over what he saw. Stonor had turned so that Marie should not see his wound, but she saw Rahaib's face, and knew at once that it was far more serious than Stonor had been prepared to admit.

Soon Stonor was in the Land-Rover being driven back to Lhalli by Rahaib. He had arrived in a small, battered Mini which, he said, he had hired in the city. Grant Williams promised to drive it back to its owner for him. Jess accompanied him, and Peter drove Marie and Jeremy back to the bungalow.

'That's the last time I go into the jungle without a gun,' Peter said grimly. He shot her a look. 'Come on, who's that fellow? A bit taciturn, isn't he?'

'He told you his name,' Marie said evasively. Since Stonor had not given Peter any information she hesitated to do so. She might annoy Stonor if she told anyone who he was—she knew him well enough by now to know that his trip to Jedhpur was probably basically a business trip. Whatever he was planning, he obviously did not want anyone to know about it.

'Yes, but who is he? What does he do? What on earth was he doing out in the jungle?'

'He's in business,' she said carefully. 'I met him through my father. They ... did business together.'

'What sort of business?' Peter asked.

'I think he's in the hotel business,' she said truthfully enough. A lie of omission was not altogether wrong, she told herself.

'But why should he be wandering around the jungle?' Peter asked insistently.

She hesitated. 'I expect he was looking for me. He knew I was out here, and my father probably asked him to look me up. Dad was a bit worried about me coming to such a remote spot.'

Peter shrugged. 'I suppose that must have been it. He was pretty annoyed about the tiger, wasn't he? A grim sort of chap. I didn't take to him.'

'He's ... rather alarming,' she agreed quietly.

Peter gave her a furtive glance. 'You ... like him, do you?'

For a moment she did not answer, then she said evasively, 'He can be a bit overwhelming at times.' It seemed an enormous understatement, but it was honest as far as it went.

# CHAPTER SEVEN

NEXT morning when Jess had gone to the stilt hut to work, Marie took Jeremy into Lhalli to do some shopping at the market, as she had promised. Rahaib and Lispa came too, so after she had brought Jeremy the new pencils he needed and a stick of chewy liquorice toffee, Marie left him with Lispa while she walked through the market to the modern hospital which the King had built some years earlier.

The tall Indian nurse at the reception desk in the low-ceilinged lobby smiled at her, listened to her question and pointed to a room at the far end of the corridor to the left.

'Mr Grey is in room 12,' she said. A mischievous twinkle came into her eyes. 'Be warned, Miss Brinton, he is in a very bad mood. The nurse who took him his medicine an hour ago came out looking as if she, too, had been mauled by a tiger.'

Marie laughed. 'As bad as that?'

'He is most irascible man,' the receptionist said sadly. 'But men make bad patients—we all know that. They hate being in bed for hours with nothing to do.'

'How is his shoulder?' Marie asked.

The receptionist glanced at her carefully. 'He is as well as can be expected. He was lucky to get off so lightly. A tiger can kill quickly. He might have lost the use of his arm had he not been rescued so soon.'

Marie walked down the corridor and tapped on the door softly. A sharp voice growled, 'What is it?'

She pushed the door open. Stonor lay in a stark little bed, his shoulder swathed in bandages, the dark head turned to survey her.

'Come in and shut the door,' he said after a moment, his voice expressionless.

Marie obeyed and came towards the bed, depositing on his little bedside table the bag of fruit she had brought him. He stared at it.

'What's this? Occupational therapy?'

'Fruit,' she said. 'I hear you've been giving the nurses a lot of trouble.'

His dark brows lifted ironically. 'Gossiping with the nurses, were you? Did they tell you that you saved my life?'

She flushed. 'Nonsense.'

'It's true,' he said crisply. 'Another minute and I would have been a tiger's dinner.'

'Peter would have done something,' she said.

He laughed drily. 'Peter? That's his name, is it? A rather ineffectual young man, isn't he? He ran around the beast trying to drive it off with a stick ...'

'It was his pistol I shot at it with,' she told him.

'Oh, you shot at it, did you?' he mocked. 'Well, I hate to tell you, in the circumstances, but you missed.'

'It drove him off, anyway,' she said indignantly. 'You're very ungrateful.'

'Is that what you want? Gratitude?' He lay back, watching her with amused eyes.

She looked at him directly. 'What are you doing here, Stonor? Why did you come to Jedhpur?'

'Why do you think?' he retorted.

'You tell me,' she said.

'I suppose you think I followed you out here?' he asked her softly.

Marie felt herself going pink. 'Did you?'

He laughed. 'As a matter of fact I'm here on business. It's a very delicate matter, and I don't want any hint of it to get out for the moment, so by all means let everyone believe I followed you here.' His eyes mocked her again. 'I don't mind being gossiped about as a lovesick suitor.'

'Perhaps I mind being made the object of gossip,' she pointed out. 'How do I know you really are here on business? You've told me so many lies I don't know what to believe.'

His face hardened. 'I'm not lying now. Very well, I'll tell you. I'm after the hotel concession for the new National Park. This place could be a great tourist attraction if it was built up in the right way. Safari holidays are fashionable. We could make a lot of money here.'

'So that's it,' she said, flatly.

'That's it,' he murmured, watching her face.

'You turn everything to your own advantage, don't you?' she accused him. 'You hadn't even thought of the idea when I told you I was coming here. You got the idea from what I told you about the place.'

'That's right,' he agreed.

'Have you seen the King?'

'I can't approach him directly,' Stonor said. 'It would cause too much talk.' He looked at her sideways. 'I need a go-between.'

'And that's why you came looking for me yesterday,' she said quietly.

'And met a tiger,' he drawled.

'Serves you right! I wish he'd bitten your head off!'

He laughed. 'Temper, temper! What have I done to make you so angry?' The dark eyes taunted her.

Marie turned away. 'You won't get much business done lying in a hospital bed, anyway.'

'Oh, I don't know,' he drawled. 'The perfect excuse for the King to visit me ... who would question a visit to a wealthy visitor badly mauled by a tiger? You only have to see the King and let him know I want to have a few quiet words with him.'

'Just like that?'

He grinned at her. 'Just like that, Marie.'

'And if it's embarrassing for me to have it known that you followed me here? That doesn't matter?'

He was silent, watching her face intently. 'Is there something I don't know? Like another man, for instance?'

She looked down, biting her lip. 'It's possible, isn't it?'

'This Peter?'

She shrugged. 'Possibly.'

'For God's sake, Marie,' he exploded, 'either you're involved with him or you aren't. Make yourself clear.'

She was blazingly angry with him for using her as a shield in one of his business deals. Her pride and her feelings were both hurt. At least, she thought bitterly, she could retrieve her pride by lying to him.

'All right,' she said stiffly, 'I don't want Peter to think I'm involved with you.'

For a moment Stonor didn't move. Then he said grimly, 'That's a pity. Because I'm going to need your co-operation.'

'Who do you think you are, riding roughshod over other people's lives in this way? Why on earth should I help you?'

He made a shrugging movement and gave a stifled groan, his free hand rising to his bandaged shoulder. She was anxious, moving to help him. He waved her away with a grim face.

Marie drew back, watching him, seeing the new whiteness in his lean face. 'Oh, very well,' she said wearily. 'I'll try to see the King.'

'You'll need an excuse,' he said. 'You can't just walk in there and demand that he visit me.'

'I'll be discreet,' she promised irritably.

'What will you say?' he demanded.

'Leave it to me,' she said, turning towards the door.

'Thank you for the fruit,' he called as she opened it.

She looked back angrily. Stonor grinned at her and lifted one hand in farewell, and she closed the door with a bang.

The receptionist watched her walk back and grinned at her. 'Did he bite your head off too? You look as though you've had a bad time in there.'

'He's impossible!' Marie said with feeling. 'I suppose being one of the richest men in the world makes him above ordinary human customs like courtesy.'

The nurse's eyes widened. 'Is he really one of the richest men in the world?'

'Oh, yes,' Marie said with a shrug. 'Didn't you know? He's a multi-millionaire. But he's travelling incognito.'

'What is he doing in Jedhpur?' the nurse asked.

Marie made a little fluttering movement with her

hands. 'He came to see me,' she confessed, looking down with a little smile. Then she walked out, feeling the nurse's eyes on her back with intense curiosity.

Having sown the first seed of her plan, she got Rahaib to drive her to the palace and asked to see the Princess Aissa. She sent in a note, reminding the Princess that she was the governess of Mrs Cunningham's little boy. Aziz's plan to bring the two of them together had not yet been fulfilled, but Marie was sure the Princess would see her.

After a wait of half an hour, she was conducted down endless marble corridors to a beautifully furnished room where she found the Princess seated on a silk-cushioned couch. Slight, graceful and dark-eyed, the Princess gave her a friendly smile, holding out her coral-tipped fingers.

'Miss Brinton? Aziz has told me about you. I am so pleased to meet you. I would have arranged a meeting before today, but I have been away on a visit and have just returned. Please be seated. Will you take tea?'

'Thank you,' said Marie, seating herself on a low silk-upholstered stool next to the table.

The Princess clapped her hands, and a plump woman in blue silk hurried through the door and bowed.

'Tea,' the Princess commanded.

A few moments later the woman returned with the large silver tea tray. She poured tea for them both, handed a plate of tiny sweetmeats to Marie, and was then dismissed by Princess Aissa.

'Now,' said the Princess, 'can I do something to help you?' Her dark eyes smiled, 'I suspect your visit was not entirely altruistic.'

Marie flushed. 'I would have come anyway, but it's true that I need your help. A friend of mine is in the hospital ...'

'Mr Grey,' the Princess nodded.

Marie looked at her in surprise. 'You've heard about it?'

'My brother had a report immediately it happened.' The Princess smiled at her. 'Dear Miss Brinton, Lhalli is not London. Nothing happens here that is not observed. My brother likes to keep his fingers on the pulses of the country. The arrival of a very rich and famous man causes interest wherever it happens, and when he is mauled by a tiger that is serious. My brother heard about it at once.' The Princess glanced at her, her dark eyes amused. 'He also gathered that Mr Grey's visit was apparently in connection with you, Miss Brinton. Mr Grey's first action on arrival was to find out where you were living and set out for the bungalow. Then he apparently followed you into the jungle. So my brother deduced that his visit here was therefore a personal one.'

Marie flushed and looked down. 'Yes, but ...'

'Otherwise my brother would have gone to the hospital himself to see if there was anything he could do,' the Princess went on, nibbling at a sweetmeat. 'However, he felt he might be intruding if he went there today.'

Marie hesitated. It was difficult to phrase her next remark. How could she ask the King to visit Stonor without betraying Stonor's reason for being in Jedhpur? His real reason?

'My brother was afraid Mr Grey might be annoyed if

he knew how much interest his arrival had caused,' the Princess added. She smiled at Marie. 'Even the very rich have a right to privacy where matters of the heart are concerned.'

Marie felt her face glowing. 'I ... I'm sure Stonor would be very glad to see the King,' she said nervously. 'I have my job to do, your Highness. I must be at the bungalow with the little boy. Stonor is alone all day.'

The Princess paused to stare at her. 'Were you hoping I could find someone to take your place looking after Mrs Cunningham's son? I am sure Lispa would be very happy...'

'No,' Marie said quickly, 'thank you. It isn't that. But ... Mr Grey does not have a telephone in his room, you see. He needs to make telephone calls overseas rather urgently. I wondered if one could be installed ... he has so many business matters to look after, you know...'

The Princess considered. 'I am sure something could be arranged. Indeed, I don't see why Mr Grey should not be transferred from the hospital to a room in the palace. He could have daily visits from his doctor here, and a nurse could accompany him. Do you think that would suit him?'

Marie was certain it would, but she said courteously, 'Oh, I don't think we could put you to so much trouble ...'

'It would be no trouble,' the Princess shrugged. 'Mr Grey is a very wealthy and influential man, Miss Brinton, and we need the help and support of men like him. My brother would be delighted to have him to stay with us. We thought of it at once. We only hesitated because we were not sure of his wishes.'

'I think he would be most grateful for your kindness,' Marie said quietly.

The Princess smiled at her. 'And you could visit him as often as you wished. Lispa will look after the little boy. I would be very pleased to see you here. I have so. few friends, and I miss the life I led in Europe. Now that I am back home I am so constricted. I think Aziz told you how we feel . . .'

'Your cousin did mention something of the kind,' Marie admitted.

Aissa's small face lit up. 'Aziz is always so thoughtful!'

Marie remembered what Rahaib had said about him, and she wondered how well the Princess knew her charming but irresponsible cousin. She listened as Aissa poured out her longings for Europe, her fear of an arranged marriage to someone she could not love.

'Love has another meaning here. It stands for duty and family affection. Romantic love is suspect.'

'I'm sure your brother would not force you to marry someone you didn't like,' Marie soothed.

Aissa sighed. 'My brother is not a free agent. His Council is divided. My uncle and his friends wish to halt our movement towards progress. They want to stop the clock. They fear our new ideas.'

'And Prince Aziz? He is on your side?'

Aissa smiled, her dark eyes eloquent. 'Yes, Aziz is with us.'

Watching her, Marie suddenly guessed that the Princess was in love with her cousin. Was he, perhaps, also in love with her? He had shown much concern for her, yet she had felt at the time that Aziz was not acting solely out of cousinly affection, and she was sure that Rahaib had suspected something behind his desire to help Aissa find freedom.

She left the palace, much relieved to have had her task made so much easier. Now Stonor would have plenty of time in which to talk to the King. She determined that she would not visit him. He had played his last trick on her.

She spent that evening with Peter, who arrived unannounced at the bungalow, and invited himself to supper. Jess, amused, left them alone after the meal.

Peter moved to sit beside Marie on the sofa, his arm stealing along behind her shoulder. 'You're awfully pretty,' he told her awkwardly.

She smiled at him. 'Thank you.' But she felt no interest in him whatever. The shadow of Stonor Grey cast every other man into the shade. Even now, sitting here beside Peter, her only thought was somehow connected with Stonor, wondering what he was doing, what he was thinking.

Peter leaned towards her and she watched him abstractedly, hardly caring whether he kissed her or not. When his mouth clumsily sought and found her lips she sat there without responding, as if she was in a trance. Why should I let Stonor come between me and life like this? she asked herself furiously. On an impulse she slipped her arms around Peter's neck and began to kiss him back, curling close to him.

'Oh, Marie,' Peter breathed as he released her. 'You're fantastic! I could be crazy about you ...'

She laughed. 'Oh, could you?'

'Don't tease,' he said sulkily.

He moved to kiss her again, but she averted her head. 'No,' she said, already sorry she had encouraged him. 'No more...'

'You're like a will-o'-the-wisp,' he complained. 'One can't get hold of you.'

'Time you went,' she retorted. 'I have to get up early in the morning. Young Jeremy rises with the dawn, and I need my beauty sleep.'

'I suppose I ought to be going,' he said reluctantly. 'I have to get up early too. When can I see you again?'

'You know where I am,' she said lightly. 'Tomorrow Jess and I are going out to the stilt hut again, but this time alone—no men invited. Jeremy didn't see much of the animals, thanks to our little excitement.'

'How is that chap going on?' Peter asked, staring at her.

'Fine, as far as I know,' she said evasively.

Next day Jess, Marie and Jeremy drove out to the stilt hut and spent the daylight hours there. Jess worked while Marie and Jeremy watched the animals, then Marie prepared their picnic meal and they all sat down on the straw mats inside the hut to eat it.

'I'm afraid that tiger has a short life expectancy since he attacked your friend,' Jess sighed.

'What do you mean?'

'The villagers are nervous about him. He's too close to their huts. Sometimes a tiger takes a child—and they're all terrified it will be one of their children. They've asked the King to arrange a tiger hunt, Rahaib says. They want him shot.'

'Oh, poor tiger,' Marie said sadly. 'He was so beautiful, too.'

Jess smiled at her. 'You can't blame them. It's unusual for a tiger to come so close to a village—they usually hunt deep in the jungle and keep away from men. This one must be a man-eater, and they're too dangerous to be allowed to live. Usually, they run away from men, but this one deliberately attacked. That makes him savage.'

Jeremy was peering down river, his straw hat crooked on his little head. 'Mum, what's that?' he demanded.

Jess peered over his shoulder. 'What's what, darling?'

He pointed. 'That black hump, in the water down there.'

Jess laughed. 'That, my darling, is a rhinoceros wallowing in one of the shallow pools at the edge of the river. See, there's his horn sticking up . . .'

'At least men don't hunt rhinoceros for their skin,' Marie said with a sigh. 'The beautiful animals always seem to be hunted.'

'Oh, men hunt the rhino, too,' Jess said sadly.

'What for?' Jeremy demanded. 'Do they make handbags out of him like they do with the crocodile?'

Jess shook her head wryly. 'No, they saw off his horns and use them in a sort of medicine.' She glanced sideways at Marie and added quietly, 'They believe it acts as an aphrodisiac. Rhino horn costs five hundred pounds a ton.'

'Nothing is safe, is it?' Marie muttered.

They were tired when they drove back home. Marie put Jeremy to bed early, his small body limp in her arms, and then went along to Jess to join her for dinner. Later she washed her hair, had a bath and went to bed early. She heard Jess turn in about half an hour later.

Next day, she and Lispa went to the market with Jeremy, to buy a chicken and some fruit. Jeremy watched a market conjuror with excited fascination. He found the exotic sights and smells of the market enthralling even now and enjoyed nothing so much as a visit there.

After lunch, she settled down on the verandah with Jeremy to play snap. Jeremy thoroughly enjoyed this and became hysterical with laughter. Jess came home early because a sudden brief storm had made the stilt hut temporarily uninhabitable. The rain had driven in through the open sides and left it awash with water which was immediately filled with frogs and insects driven to shelter from the storm outside. Her Land-Rover was splashed with mud so thick and dark it looked like a mud pie on wheels. Jess herself was filthy and immediately took a bath.

They were just finishing dinner when Rahaib entered the room with his customary impassive expression. He bowed, glancing at Marie.

'A message from the palace,' he said, handing her an envelope with great gravity.

She opened it, guessing who it would be from. Stonor had not wasted words. The scrawled, impatient writing merely said: Come here at once. There was not even a signature.

Marie looked up, flushing. 'How did the message get here?'

'By car,' Rahaib told her. 'It waits outside to take you to the palace.'

'To the palace?' Jess raised her brows. 'To see the King?'

'No,' said Marie. 'Stonor Grey wants to see me.'

'Is he at the palace now? He must have some pull.' Jess stood up, pushing back her chair. 'It's rather late to issue invitations, though.'

Marie hesitated, longing to say she would not go, but knew she could not rest in peace until she had discovered what Stonor wanted.

'I think I should go,' she said. 'He may need help.'

Jess shrugged, 'Do as you like, Marie.' She sauntered away, losing interest, and Marie glanced down at her denims and shirt.

'I must change first,' she told Rahaib.

'Yes, my lady,' he said. He did not approve of her jeans—he made that clear every time he saw them, without saying a word.

She went to her room and found a cream silk dress which looked very good on her without making it seem as if she had particularly dressed up for this visit. She brushed her hair up into a chignon, applied new make-up and put on shoes which matched the dress.

The car sped to the palace along the dark, dusty roads. In the distance a jackal howled, making the hair stand up on the back of her neck. The headlights lit up the road ahead, making ghostly circles in the white dust.

When they entered the market area Marie was surprised to find it still crowded, despite the late hour. The stalls were lit by naphtha flares. The hawkers still shouted their wares, and the smell of food was stronger than ever. Only the old women no longer gossiped around the well, and there were fewer children about to stare at the car.

She was escorted through the marble corridors of the palace to a room on an upper floor. The servant indicated the door, bowed and took up a crouching position opposite it, apparently prepared to sit and wait until she appeared again.

Marie tapped on the door.

'Come in,' Stonor called.

She went into the room and found him lying on a low couch, his head and shoulders cushioned, the shutters covering the windows and a lamp burning softly beside him, making a dim circle of yellow light around the couch.

She stared at him hungrily, tracing the shadows under his eyes, the hint of weariness in his posture. He still looked ill, but there had been an improvement since she last saw him.

'Well, come here,' he said sharply. 'I can't see you over there.'

She moved over towards him, halting a few feet from the couch. 'What did that rather peremptory message mean?' she enquired coldly.

'What do you mean by staying away from me for two days?' he demanded in return.

Her heart thudded. 'Did you expect me to haunt your sickbed?' she asked huskily.

'I expected you to keep up our little fiction about my presence in Jedhpur being on your account,' he retorted.

'Oh,' she murmured, feeling angrily disillusioned. 'That's it.'

He eyed her enigmatically. 'Don't loom over me like that. Sit down.'

Marie looked around, but there was nowhere to sit. He

patted the couch invitingly. 'Here ...' he commanded.

She hesitated.

'For God's sake, sit down, girl!' he barked.

She sat down where he had pointed, and Stonor lay back, relaxing, his dark eyes fixed on her face.

'What have you been doing with yourself?' he asked.

She shrugged. 'Nothing much. Today I did the shopping and then played with Jeremy.'

'And yesterday?'

'I spent the day at the marshes watching the animals feed with Jess and Jeremy,' she told him, then added deliberately, 'In the evening I had dinner with Peter.'

The dark eyes narrowed. 'How romantic! How far has the affair got? Does he make love to you?'

She flushed hotly. 'We've kissed,' she flung defiantly.

He bared his teeth in a grim smile. 'Now I wonder why you feel the need to be so belligerent about it?'

'You make me nervous,' she said defensively.

'Do I?' he asked very softly. 'Why?'

She shifted uneasily. 'I don't know. You just do.'

He put his free hand over her fingers. 'Stop fidgeting like that. You're like a cat on hot bricks.'

The touch of his hand made her bones turn to water. 'How ... how are you getting on with the King?' she asked.

'It was easier than I'd imagined,' he said calmly. 'As it turned out, he needs me as much as I need him. He lacks capital, and he was eager to work out a deal. I think we shall both make a lot of money.'

'And Jedhpur? Will that benefit?' she asked cynically.

The dark eyes lifted to her face. 'Sarcasm doesn't suit you. Yes, Jedhpur will benefit a great deal. It needs investment. It needs industry. It needs tourism. I'll supply all three.'

'Then if you've already made your deal you don't need to keep up the pretence of being here to see me,' she said.

'More than ever,' he told her. 'The King wants to keep our deal a secret for the time being. He's afraid of trouble from the conservative element, and he wants to present them with a fait accompli.'

Marie tried to withdraw her fingers from his grip, but he tightened it. 'Let me go, Stonor,' she said breathlessly.

'No,' he murmured.

Their eyes battled, then hers dropped away. Once again she felt that strange, weak helplessness which she had first felt when he kissed her; overwhelmed by the realisation that she was physically his inferior, unable to win a fight against him.

'I can't stay much longer,' she said. 'It's a long drive back.'

'I like that dress,' he merely replied. 'The colour suits you. It's gently understating your femininity.'

She looked at him through her lashes. 'Thank you.'

'Don't do that,' he said abruptly. 'You don't need tricks like that.'

'Tricks?' She was blazingly angry. 'Why, you . . .'

He laughed at her expression. 'My dear girl, I've known too many females to be taken in by any of those age-old tricks: the eyelash fluttering, the sidelong glances, the tossed head . . .'

'How about the slap in the face?' she said furiously.

His mouth twitched. 'Try it and see.'

'I bet you'd hit me back,' she said sulkily.

'You'd win your bet,' he answered mockingly.

Marie moved to rise, but he was pinioning her down with his one hand and she dared not struggle too hard for hear of hurting him.

'I've got to go,' she said crossly.

'Kiss me goodnight, then,' he said softly.

She glared at him. 'I certainly will not!'

'Walls have eyes in this place,' he said. 'I'm pretty sure that servant doesn't speak much English, but I know he watches me through the keyhole because I've seen him at it.' The dark eyes flicked over her mockingly. 'So be a good girl and give me a kiss.'

Marie hesitated, then bent slowly forward. His hand left her fingers and came up to clasp her head, pulling her down towards him, until their lips met. The kiss was gentle for a moment, his mouth warmly coaxing. Then fire blazed between them and she felt her self-control slip from her like a straw in a tidal flood.

Against her mouth he whispered, 'You drive me crazy, do you know that?'

'Do I?' Her voice was husky, she pulled away from him to stare down into the brightness of his eyes. 'I hadn't noticed.'

'You're too busy convincing yourself you hate me to notice anything,' he drawled.

'What are you saying? What do you really mean?' She knew she was on the point of tears. He was tormenting her with this cat-and-mouse game, aware that she found him irresistible, enjoying the ability to arouse her whenever he wished. 'I never understand you, Stonor.'

'Oh, you understand me,' he drawled, kissing the

curve of her naked arm inside her elbow. 'You know how I feel about you.'

'I don't ... I wish I did ...'

His dark eyes grew hot as he stared at her, his mouth deliberately lingering on her white skin, travelling slowly down towards her wrist.

'I want to take you to bed,' he said thickly. 'You're lovely and desirable and I want you. It's my misfortune that this time I've fallen for a girl who's only half alive, who prefers to be treated like a pretty doll than to be treated as a woman ...'

'This time?' She picked up the words jealously. 'Yes, how many other times have there been, Stonor? How many other women in your life?'

'Did you imagine I'd led the life of a monk?'

'Any man I married would have to intend to be faithful to me for the rest of his life,' she said miserably.

'Were we talking about marriage?' he asked gravely.

She flushed. 'I know you weren't, but I'm not going to bed with you as casually as I would choose a hat, Stonor. When I fall in love it's going to be for keeps.'

'And I don't qualify,' he murmured.

'You don't play the game by my rules,' she said.

'Love has no rules, darling,' he said.

'It has where I'm concerned.'

'You've a lot to learn.'

'Not from you!' she flung.

'From who, then? This ineffective young archaeologist you've picked up? He looked as inexperienced as you are.'

'Then perhaps we'll learn together,' she retorted, standing up and moving away towards the door.

Stonor swore under his breath and she looked back at him. 'Careful! At your age you have to watch your blood pressure.'

'Vixen!' he muttered.

'Goodnight, Stonor.'

'Come back tomorrow,' he said quickly as she opened the door, but she did not answer.

# CHAPTER EIGHT

EACH time she visited Stonor, Marie afterwards took tea
with Princess Aissa, either in her private apartments or
in a small walled garden shut away from prying masculine eyes on the women's side of the palace. This part of
the building, Marie soon realised, was far more elaborately decorated, far more beautifully furnished than the
public rooms only visited by men. The Kings of Jedhpur,
in past years, had created a scented, silk-draped paradise
for their queens. Marie gazed around these marble-
floored, gilded cages and wondered what it had felt like to
be the bird of paradise imprisoned here. She remembered
that Stonor had once threatened her with harem life—on
that evening when he played kidnapper for his own
amusement. He had said that she was already, in fact, the
prisoner of luxury; indulged, petted and spoilt but shut
away from ordinary life. In a sense she knew it was true.
Her father had protected her from the problems and
pains of life, but in protecting her had walled her up
away from the free winds of the world. Now she knew
just how much she had missed.

She had looked at her hands with dismay, hating the
softness and whiteness of her unscathed palms. Lispa's
brown hands were rough from work, and they had a
beauty of their own, a beauty and dignity Marie envied.
She longed to have Lispa's deft agility, her quick graceful
skill in household tasks. She longed to have Jess's artistic

skills, too, or to use her brain in the challenge of industry, or learn even any basic industrial skills.

Anything, in fact, but be useless.

The job Jess had given her was really only a space in which to find her true métier. She spent hours thinking about the future. What could she learn to do? What could she train for? Nursing? That had an appeal. You did not need to be brilliant in order to take up nursing, and her education had been a sound one. Or should she go to a teacher training college? She rejected that idea after some thought as it did not appeal to her. She rejected a business training, too. One by one she considered various jobs and always came back to the idea of nursing. It was an alarming prospect, but she wanted to do something really useful, and it seemed the best way to do that.

She discussed the problem with Princess Aissa and Aziz, during their tea parties. Somehow Aziz always contrived to be on hand for these occasions. He would knock on the door, look surprised and say cheerfully, 'Well, well, Miss Brinton . . . may I come in?'

Aissa would turn her sleek black head on the long column of her swanlike neck and the almond eyes would smile at him, the corners of the pale pink mouth turn up.

Now and then, as she passed him a cup or a small sweet cake, her fragile, pink-tipped fingers would brush his hand. Once, as Marie was gazing with enchanted eyes at the intense blue of the afternoon sky, she turned back suddenly and caught Aziz kissing Aissa's fingertips, his adoring eyes on the Princess's shy, averted face. Marie felt her own heart quiver at the look on their faces. There was something intensely exciting about the small gesture.

In their formal world Aziz's delicate kiss took on the quality of an explosion of passion.

When she met Lord Hathni, as she sometimes did, leaving the palace with Aziz beside her, talking lightly as they walked, she felt herself tense with alarm at the quick, shrewd glance she received from the Prime Minister's eyes. Aziz would bow his head, his palms together, in that graceful gesture of submissive greeting, and Lord Hathni would give him the same shrewd glance.

Once it occurred to her that Lord Hathni suspected Aziz of having an interest in her. She gently suggested this idea to Aziz, who grinned shamelessly.

'But of course he does! He is a man. He knows that no young man of passion could see your enchanting beauty and be unmoved.'

Marie saw the twinkle in his eye as he made this teasing remark. 'Unless, of course, he happened to be far more interested in another girl?' she suggested.

Aziz looked at her sideways, his slanting eyes amused. 'That would, of course, make a difference.'

She hesitated. 'But your father doesn't seem worried by the interest he appears to think you have in me,' she said with some embarrassment.

Aziz looked down at the marble floor, and for a second she thought that he, too, was embarrassed. Then he looked up and shrugged. 'Miss Brinton, my father does not believe I would so jeopardise my position as to marry an English girl,' he said gently.

She flushed, then laughed. 'I see. He trusts your common sense.'

Aziz spread his brown hands. 'Yes.'

'Then what does he...' She broke off, flushing, even more hotly. 'Oh!'

Aziz looked at her uneasily, seeing her eyes grow stormy. 'My father may put what construction he wishes upon the evidence, but we know, do we not, that he is wrong? That is all that matters.'

'Not to me,' she said indignantly. 'Your father can't be allowed to go on imagining that I'm permitting you to make love to me ... I'm sorry if it interferes with your little conspiracy, but in future I can't allow my reputation to be used as a shield for you and the Princess...'

Aziz stiffened and gazed at her angrily. 'The Princess and I have never seen each other alone, Miss Brinton. Either you or one of her women have been present on all occasions. Do not suspect anything else. I give you my word that nothing I have ever done could harm the Princess.'

She looked at him directly, her blue eyes wide. 'Except that what you're doing is going to come out, sooner or later, and then there'll be terrible trouble for her.'

Aziz frowned, biting his lip. 'What else can we do? Our lives are made intolerable by the present situation. We are snatching what tiny crumbs of happiness we can. The future is grim for both of us.' He looked at her, his eyes miserable. 'Did you know that I am betrothed to a girl of thirteen, Miss Brinton? My father arranged the match ten years ago. I have never seen her. I will not see her for two years. Then it will only be on my wedding day, when the veil is removed from her head after we have taken our seven steps around the fire.'

'Seven steps around the fire?' she asked in bewilderment.

He nodded. 'The fire is the centre of our wedding ceremony, you see. We take seven steps around the fire, and on the last step the ceremony is complete. We are man and wife. Only then does the bride throw back her veil and reveal her face.'

Marie felt sorry for him. It was a terrifying thought ... to be tied for life to an unknown person, committed to them whatever their character—a form of Russian roulette which could have lifelong consequences.

'It has been our custom for so long,' Aziz sighed. 'My father honestly cannot understand why I resist it. He only met my mother on their wedding day, and it is true that theirs was a very happy marriage until the day she died.'

'Perhaps your marriage will be happy too,' Marie said gently. 'Surely if you've known about it for so long, you must have adjusted to the idea?'

'Aissa is my beloved,' Aziz said quietly. 'She always has been. In Europe we saw each other frequently, and we learnt to love. Now that we are back here life has grown bitter for us.'

Rahaib was waiting for her outside the palace. He had been shopping in the market for a gift for Lispa, who had just told him that she was again expecting a child. Rahaib was unusually gay, singing softly under his breath as he drove back to the bungalow. A package lay on the seat beside him. It was, he had informed Marie proudly, some fine silk from which Lispa could make herself a new sari.

'Red as the pomegranate, red for passion,' he said delightedly. 'Gold as the sun, gold for joy.'

'That's very poetic, Rahaib,' Marie said teasingly.

He smiled at her over his shoulder. 'Lispa is a good wife. She has borne me three sons. Perhaps she will bear me a fourth.'

'Wouldn't you like a girl this time?'

'If the gods desire it I will have a girl,' Rahaib said carelessly, and added. 'But I wish for a son.'

Marie laughed. 'You're a chauvinist,' she said.

He was puzzled. 'What does that mean?'

'It means you think boys are more important than girls,' she told him.

'They are,' he said in bewilderment. 'Look around you. It is obvious.'

'Yes,' she said drily, 'I'm afraid you are right.'

Rahaib flicked a glance at her apologetically. 'In your world I know it is different, but here we do things as we have always done.'

As he turned back to the road he gave a soft exclamation of surprise. 'There is a car across the road ...'

'Someone has broken down,' said Marie, leaning forward to stare ahead.

A dark car was slewed across in their path, and beside it a young man in a thin shirt and trousers was waving at them. Rahaib slowed down and stopped just in front of the car.

The young man came round to speak to Rahaib. 'Please, sir, would you look at my engine? It is not working.' He spoke in heavily accented English, but he looked Indian.

Rahaib gave him a scornful glance. 'Certainly I will look,' he replied. 'You should learn to mend your car before you begin to drive it, though.' He climbed out and walked to the other car. The bonnet was raised already, and he bent over to look at it. Immediately the young man raised a heavy wooden club and struck him down with one carefully placed blow on the head.

Marie gave a scream of dismay, as Rahaib slumped forward silently. The young man dragged his body away, flung him on to the side of the road. Marie fumbled for the keys in the dashboard, but before she could move over and start the engine there were several young men climbing into the vehicle beside her. One of them held a small gun.

She looked at them, shivering. This was no romantic game, like the one Stonor had played. This was real.

'We must blindfold and gag you, miss,' one of them said. 'Please make no trouble. We do not want to hurt you.'

Their eyes were implacable. She looked round at their faces and felt icy cold.

One of them bound a piece of cloth over her eyes, then stuffed a handkerchief into her mouth. Then she was led away, stumbling awkwardly, and placed in the other car. The engine started and the car swung round, churning dust and small stones, and drove away at breakneck speed.

The drive lasted for what seemed to her a very long time. When the car stopped at last, she was asked to get out. Guided by the hand of one of the young men, she was led into a house, then she heard the door close behind her.

The gag and blindfold were removed, and she put up a hand to her trembling lips. Pieces of lint were adhering to her inner mouth. The young men gestured for her to walk into a small room, and Marie obeyed silently, staring around her. Shutters had been placed over the window. The room was lit by an oil lamp. The only furniture was a small camp bed covered by some blankets and a pillow; two wooden chairs of great age, a low round table and a heavily carved chest with a domed top.

'Why have you brought me here?' she asked shakily, looking at the men.

The one with the gun said politely, 'You are a hostage, Miss Brinton.'

'A hostage?' She felt incredulous disbelief. 'For what?'

'We have grievances which we wish to have heard,' he said. 'Until they are heard, you will remain here.'

'But I'm nothing to do with your country,' she protested.

'You are the woman of the chairman of Unex,' he said clumsily. 'All of Jedhpur know you visit him at the palace. He will wish you to be released. He will persuade the King to hear us.'

'What if it doesn't work out like that?' she asked. 'What if the King refuses to come to terms?'

They looked at each other, then the man with the gun shrugged. 'Too bad for you.'

Marie sat down suddenly on the edge of the bed. Her legs had turned to water.

The men withdrew towards the door, staring at her. They had a quick, whispered conference, then the one with a gun came back to her and said roughly, 'You will wish to have a woman to help you. One is coming, but is not here yet. Is there anything you want?'

She glanced at him. Not quite inhuman, she thought wryly. 'I would like some water,' she said quietly.

He gestured to one of the others, who went out and

came back with a large earthenware jug of water and a tin mug.

Marie drank thirstily, then began to wonder if she had been wise to drink unboiled water. One of the first things she had learnt since arriving was that it was dangerous to drink unboiled water since so many of the rivers were heavily polluted.

'When the woman gets here, there will be food,' the man with the gun said.

One of the others said something in his own tongue, and the man with the gun looked at her.

'It will be curry. We have no English food.'

Marie smiled at him slightly. 'I eat your food every day,' she said. 'I'm quite used to it, thank you.'

He seemed taken aback, as if her courtesy disturbed him. After a moment he and the others moved out of the room and closed the door. She got up and went to the windows. There were small holes in the shutters. She peered through them and saw only blue sky.

Hearing sounds outside, she quickly returned to the bed and sat down on the edge again, her back very upright.

The door opened and the man with the gun came in, his thin dark face alert. Behind him came a young woman in a gay blue sari, her forehead decorated with the red mark Marie recognised as the sign of a married woman. She was carrying a large earthenware bowl covered with a white cloth. A savoury smell floated from it. She carefully laid it on the low table, then turned and made a polite bow.

'Will you eat?' Her English was careful and precise but not fluent.

'Thank you,' said Marie, forcing a smile.

She felt instinctively that she must try to make friends with them. It was useless to protest or make a fuss. They had a grimly determined look which made such protests merely pointless.

The young woman went out and returned with a plate. She laid it on the table, gestured to one of the chairs. 'Please sit.'

Marie obediently sat down, and the young woman took away the white cloth. Marie looked hungrily at the meal revealed—spicy, thick and fragrant, the curried lamb lay in one half of the bowl, white rice lay in the other. The young woman took up a ladle, enquiringly looked at Marie.

'What?' she asked thickly.

Marie pointed to both curry and rice. The young woman ladled some of each on to a plate. Then she paused, biting her lip, and asked quietly, *'Tarkeean?'*

Marie looked at her, recognising the word, trying to remember what it meant. The young man with the gun behind her said, 'Do you wish to have vegetable curry also?'

Marie shook her head. 'Thank you, no.'

The young woman handed her a spoon and stepped back from the table. Marie looked round at the two of them.

'Aren't you going to eat with me?'

The young woman stared at her, then looked at the young man. He spoke quickly in his own tongue. She made a frightened motion of her hands. *'Kubbee— kubbee nahin!'*

Never, no, never, thought Marie, translating mentally.

She knew enough of the language to recognise that phrase. Why would the woman not eat with her? she wondered.

The young man looked at her and shrugged. 'She will not eat.'

'Why won't she eat with me?' Marie asked him quietly.

His eyes shifted. 'It is forbidden to eat at the table with one whom one may kill,' he said uneasily.

Marie shivered. 'I see.' There was something chillingly direct about the way they said that.

Her appetite had vanished suddenly, but she forced herself to eat. The food was good and as she ate she recovered some of her spirits.

Afterwards she lay down on the bed and slept. The others withdrew, leaving her alone in the lamplit room. She heard the chirping of crickets outside, a lively, cheerful sound at most times, but tonight it had a melancholy which depressed her.

If only she could see the outside world, she thought. The silence surrounding the building made her suspect that they were in an isolated place. Why would they not let her see outside?

The next morning she lay on the bed with her eyes open listening to the sounds of cows mooing somewhere in the distance. They were in the country somewhere, then, she thought, not in Lhalli.

The door opened and the young woman came in with a bowl of warm water. She gestured to it. 'Wash...' She hung a rough cotton towel over the chair, placed a cake of scented soap on a small bowl. Marie had already discovered that the only sanitation was primitive, and she was relieved to find that she was going to be allowed to wash and brush her hair.

The day wore on slowly. She attempted to talk to her female guard, but found that the young woman's English was extremely limited. To amuse herself, Marie began to ask her the names of objects in her own tongue, pointing to something and asking, 'What is that?'

The young woman, presumably as bored as Marie was by now, was not unwilling to play this game. She seemed to like to be Marie's teacher. Carefully she would pronounce the word, then smile slightly behind her hand at Marie's attempt to repeat it.

'I ... learn English ... at ... *madrissah* ...' she stammered once during their game.

'*Madrissah?*' Marie frowned.

The young woman nodded. '*Madrissah* in Lhalli ... King's *madrissah* ...'

'School?' Marie guessed.

The young woman smiled. 'School,' she repeated, nodding. 'Me go to the school one year ...'

Marie gestured to the woman's round red forehead mark. 'You are married woman?'

The other woman hesitated, frowning.

Marie pointed to the ring she wore on her foot, a broad gold band which shone when she moved her toes. 'Married?'

The other woman's face cleared. 'Yes ... married.'

Marie pointed to herself. 'My name ... Marie.' She pointed to the other woman. 'Your name?'

There was a slight pause, then the answer came reluctantly, 'Me ... Sarwana ...'

'You have children, Sarwana?' Marie asked her, smiling.

Sarwana's dark eyes lit up. 'One baba.'

'Boy or girl?'

'Boy child,' Sarwana said in clear English. She suddenly giggled. 'Like hymn ... Mary's boy child...'

Marie laughed back, realising that this was a joke. 'You learnt hymns at the *madrissah*?'

Sarwana made a faint grimace. 'Teacher Christian woman, sing hymns.'

Her tone was disgusted, and Marie was forced to smile. 'You did not like hymns?'

Sarwana hesitated politely then said, 'No good. Bad noise.'

Then the young man with the gun came into the room with a small notepad and a pen. He laid them on the table. 'Please write a message to Mr Grey as I dictate,' he ordered Marie.

Marie sat down and picked up the pen, staring at the paper with eyes that saw little. She was wondering what Stonor was doing now, what he was thinking, how her disappearance was affecting him.

'Write that you are a prisoner,' the young man said. 'That we will release you unharmed only when the King has released the political prisoners from jail and when he has promised to stop the negotiations with Mr Grey and end the National Park scheme for ever.'

Marie looked at him incredulously. 'You are against the National Park?'

'Write what I tell you. Do not ask me foolish questions,' he snapped, waving his gun at her.

'But the scheme will bring thousand of tourists to Jedhpur and bring employment to many of your people. Think how much money will flow into the country, money you badly need.'

'The King is turning our country into a Disneyland for rich foreigners,' he said bitterly. 'We are a land of peasants. If all these foreigners come here, the peasants will leave the land to earn big money working as servants for them, and we will lose our dignity and freedom.'

'You want Jedhpur to remain backward for ever?' she asked him quietly.

His eyes flashed. 'Write! You know nothing.'

Marie looked down at the paper and obediently wrote the message he wished to send. He snatched the paper from her and read what she had written, then he looked at her. 'It is not signed. Sign it with your name.'

The young woman spoke softly, quickly. He turned and looked at her and nodded, then he said to Marie, 'She is right. You must put some words of your own, words of love which will make this man want badly to get you back.'

Marie flushed. 'I've written what you asked me to. I will not write anything else.'

The young woman spoke again, smiling, and the man laughed. He looked at Marie rather more kindly.

'Do not be embarrassed. This must be done. Sarwana says you do not wish to have strange eyes looking at your words. See, I shall not read. You may seal envelope yourself.'

Marie looked down at the paper. Words seemed to burn on it, words she knew she would never write. If she

never saw Stonor again these would be the last things she
said to him. There was so much to say, so little that could
be said.

She wrote slowly. 'Stonor, do what you have to do.
Don't worry about me. They've been kind.' Then she
quickly sealed the envelope and handed it to the young
man. He looked at her searchingly, seeing the flush on
her cheeks, the wildness in her eyes.

Gently, he said, 'Soon you will be free. When your
man reads this he will move heaven and earth.'

When he had gone Sarwana made tea and they sat and
drank it quietly. It was served, of course, in Indian
fashion, without milk or sugar, but the liquid was refreshing, and it helped to pass the time.

Marie was allowed now to leave the little room and
walk outside. It was dark, as it had been last night when
she was given the same opportunity; so dark that she
could see nothing but the sky and the branches of the
trees which surrounded the house. The air was cool and
fragrant. It was hard to go back into the stuffiness of the
little room.

She lay down and slept later, while Sarwana departed
again, presumably to feed her baby or see to her own
house.

At dawn next morning the young man with the gun
came back. He burst into Marie's room, awaking her
from a deep and troubled sleep, and she sat up in alarm,
staring at him.

He laughed aloud, waving his arms. Sarwana stood
behind him, wreathed in smiles.

'All is agreed,' he cried delightedly. 'The prisoners are
already released. The King has announced that for the

present he will proceed no further with the National Park, and Mr Grey will leave Jedhpur without the agreement he had been negotiating.'

'You ... knew about that?' she asked, wondering how soon they would release her.

'Why else did we do all this? Oh, the King and Mr Grey tried to keep it secret, but there are patriots in the palace who objected to the plans. Now things will return to normal. The land will belong to the peasants as it has always done.'

'Or to the landlords who live in the palace?' she suggested.

He looked at her sharply and his brows jerked together. 'You do not understand how things work here.'

'When will I be released?' she asked, afraid of angering him any further.

'When it is dark,' he promised, smiling again. 'I will drive you somewhere and release you.'

The hours seemed to pass with appalling slowness while Marie waited for the moment of her release. She could not eat the food Sarwana brought her. She could only sit staring at the thin slits of light filtering through the shutters.

At last it was dark and she was led out, once more blindfolded and gagged. The drive was bumpy and unpleasant, over rough terrain; they were not, she realised, driving back the same way they had come. At last the car stopped. She was pushed out roughly, the car reversed and sped away with a grinding of gears.

Marie hurriedly untied her blindfold and removed the gag with hands that shook.

Then she stared around. She stood in the dark road on

the outskirts of a small village. The lights shone with friendly invitation just a few hundred yards away. She stumbled and ran towards them, and knocked on the first door she came to, her body trembling with the long tension of the last few days.

The door creaked slowly open and a dark face peered cautiously out at her.

'Help me,' said Marie, clinging to the door frame. Her knees were buckling under her, as if she could no longer maintain the pretence of being calmly under control.

The face withdrew. Voices chattered inside the house, then someone else came to the door. Marie held out an appealing hand, realising that they could not speak English and were more frightened of her than curious. They were amazed by the appearance of an English girl in their village at such an hour, and suspicious of her reasons for wandering about without masculine protection in the dark.

She had no money on her, no way of explaining her predicament. She held out her hands again, pleadingly. 'Lhalli,' she said. 'Me ... go to Lhalli ... Lord Hathni ...' She began to recite the names of the royal family, watching them intently.

They looked at each other, shrugging. One of them made a gesture to her, speaking loudly to the others, then he ran off into the darkness. A moment later he was back, leading a reluctant and irritable-looking mule by a rope halter. He gestured to Marie to get on the animal.

She managed to climb on to its back, looking at him nervously as he took up the halter. He turned and nodded to her, giving a shy smile.

'Lhalli,' he said, nodding. 'Lhalli...'

Then they set off into the night along the rough, rutted hill roads in the dark, moonless and haunted by the howls of jackals and the floating wail of hunting owls. Bumping and clinging to the mule for grim life, Marie felt herself wearily wishing she could just lie down and die. It was all too much for her.

The throb of an engine reached her ears suddenly, making her sit up and stare ahead. Like yellow eyes in the darkness, the headlights of a lorry shone straight at them. The peasant drew the mule to the side of the road to let the lorry pass, but instead it ground to a halt with a crash of gears, and from the back of it sprang a dozen soldiers in the palace uniform. Shouting, brandishing guns, they surrounded Marie and the peasant. The peasant cringed in terror, wailing, then Marie recognised Aziz descending from the lorry cab. He was grinning delightedly.

'My dear Miss Brinton! How glad I am to see you alive and well.' He glared at the peasant. 'You will suffer for this, animal!'

'He had nothing to do with it,' Marie assured him quickly, laying a hand on the unfortunate old man's shoulder. 'He just helped me when the others had dumped me in his village...' She told Aziz how she had been released and he spoke more kindly to the old man, drew out a handful of coins from his purse and pushed them into the old man's trembling hand. Hurriedly, with many bows, the peasant vanished into the night. Marie was not sorry to see the back of his mule, which moved much faster now that it was heading homewards, she noticed.

Aziz helped her gently into the lorry. The soldiers climbed aboard and the lorry slowly reversed. Aziz told her as they drove back to Lhalli that his cousin had been quite horrified by her kidnapping, especially since Stonor had been almost beside himself with rage and anxiety. They had searched everywhere they could think of, all the known haunts of Jedhpuri rebels, but they had found no clue as to her whereabouts.

'So the King had to give way. He could not risk your life. Mr Grey would never have been prepared to invest in our country if you had been killed.' Aziz looked at her, and smiled, relapsing into silence.

Marie was fast asleep, her head slumped against his shoulder.

# CHAPTER NINE

SHE woke up when the lorry stopped outside the palace gates. Aziz smiled at her, his glance mischievous. 'Mr Grey will be jealous when he learns you have slept on my shoulder for so long! Are you stiff? Come, let me help you down.' He lifted her down and put an arm around her as her knees gave way. 'Shall I carry you? Can you walk?'

Marie shook her head. 'It's only cramp.' She flexed her calf muscles, grimacing at the pain. 'I can walk now ...'

Lights still burned everywhere in the palace, but curious sentries stared as they passed along the marble corridors. Whispers preceded them. A soldier ran ahead to warn the King, and as they approached the royal apartments the King himself appeared in the doorway, his face tired, fully dressed.

'Miss Brinton! Heaven be praised! You are safe! Those dogs kept their word, then. We had begun to think ...' he broke off as Stonor arrived, his bandaged shoulder impeding him.

Marie looked at him, her whole being concentrated on his face. He was white, his dark eyes like bottomless wells in his face. He stood over her, staring down as if he had never seen her before, searching her face with stark intensity.

'You will wish to speak alone,' the King said quietly, clearing his throat. 'Please, use my room.'

Stonor took Marie's arm in his free hand and propelled her firmly past the King into the room. He paused before closing the door to thank the King, then shut the door and leaned against it, staring at her.

Marie was so nervous she could barely breathe. The room seemed to be full of electricity, like the sky before a storm.

'God!' Stonor groaned. 'Oh, God, Marie...'

Then he had moved towards her fast and she was in his arms, held so close she had to cling to him to stand upright. He kissed her with savage hunger, murmuring her name again and again.

'I was beginning to think they'd killed you,' he said, his voice husky. He moved his lips along her throat with feverish intensity, then returned to her mouth, parting her lips, consuming her in the flame of his own passion. 'I've been out of my mind. I wanted to tear this god-forsaken little country to shreds looking for you. I'd have paid anything, done anything, to get you back safely...'

Her blue eyes shone at him adoringly. 'Stonor,' she breathed softly. 'Darling...'

He drew back, looking down at her. 'Say that again.'

'Darling,' she repeated obediently, her hands touching the black hair at the nape of his neck, delving into the thick strands with fingers that seemed to have nerves in every pore, sensitive to his body in a way that made her shiver.

'Tell me you love me,' he demanded arrogantly.

Her happiness was so all-consuming that she was past preserving her pride or her self-respect. 'I love you, I love you,' she whispered.

'Again,' he ordered.

She lifted her blue eyes to his face again, a slightly rebellious expression in them now. 'Stonor?'

'I want to hear you say it,' he said, the lean face filled with the old arrogance.

'I think we still mean different things by the word love,' she said, suddenly saddened.

'Do we?' He brushed her upturned mouth with his lips. 'We'll have plenty of time to find out after we're married.'

Marie stood very still, her eyes fixed on his face. 'Married, Stonor?'

'Yes,' he said lightly. 'You've broken my spirit, damn you. How can I let you roam the world without protection when you keep getting yourself into trouble like this? I'd never have another moment's peace in case someone was kidnapping you. I'm afraid I'm going to have to carry on where your father left off, wrapping you in cotton wool, showering you with expensive presents, spoiling and adoring you . . .'

She took his face in both her hands, her pleading palms against his hard cheeks.

'Be serious, Stonor. Don't play one of your games.'

'I was never more serious in my life,' he retorted.

'I've said it,' she whispered. 'Why can't you?'

He was suddenly very grave, his dark eyes full of sombre thought. 'I'm afraid, Marie. Afraid of losing myself, afraid of drowning helplessly in an ocean of love. It's always been there in my nature, a weakness, the need to love with utter abandon, but I meant to fight against it for the whole of my life. I've seen what it does to men. That sort of love saps your strength. Then I met you, and when I kissed you that night in the desert I felt a terrible warning. I knew that if I let myself fall for you I would fall so far I could never get back. But by the time I'd realised it, it was already too late. I've been trying to escape from the trap ever since. I tried to convince myself you weren't worth loving, but I never quite succeeded.'

'Didn't you, Stonor?' Her blue eyes were gentle now, recognising his sincerity.

He put a hand to her golden hair, running his fingers down the silky strands. 'That hair of yours first drew my eyes—such a glorious colour! I wanted to touch it, to run my fingers through it. That was my first hint of danger. Then your blue eyes flashed at me and I felt the warning signals again—oh, I had plenty of warnings, but I ignored them all. Like a blind man walking into his fate, I let myself be caught. Perhaps I even wanted to be, secretly.'

She let her arms fall away from him and stepped back, watching him through her lowered lashes. 'You're free, Stonor. Quite free.'

He smiled grimly. 'The secret of your power, you witch, is that I no longer want to be free. For weeks I've yearned to be totally enslaved, even while I struggled against the desire to see you again. Of course I didn't come to Jedhpur to make a deal with the King—I could have done that through one of my agents. I came to see you. I had to come. I couldn't sleep at night any more. Your face was haunting my dreams, driving me mad with desire.' He reached out for her, but she evaded him.

'You still haven't said it,' she reminded him.

He stared at her, his chin raised angrily. 'I've admitted it over and over again. What else do you want?'

She did not answer, her eyes levelly fixed on his face.

He half closed his eyes and groaned. 'All right, I love you. I love you, God help me!'

Marie laughed. 'You sound as if it had been wrung from you by torture, Stonor!'

'Hasn't it?' He pulled her close with his one good hand. 'I've been denied a kiss for five full minutes. What's that but cruel torture?'

Her mouth was parted on a smile as she looked up at him. But the smile died on a gasp as his mouth descended in hard possession, melting her bones, making her shake with mounting passion. When they parted he was dark red, she was trembling.

'We've got to get back to England and get married before I lose all my last shreds of self-control,' he said grimly.

'I can't leave Jess without anyone to look after Jeremy,' she protested. 'He needs constant care.'

'We'll fly someone out to take your place,' he said easily, brushing the problem aside. 'That woman who works there can take over until the new girl arrives. After all, she's been looking after the child while you were away.' He looked at her gently. 'Jess was very worried about you, you know. She was intent on blaming herself for what happened. She thought that if she'd never brought you out here it wouldn't have happened, which, in a way, I suppose, is true.'

'Poor Jess,' she said. 'We must go to the bungalow right away and tell her the good news.'

'I think the King wants to ask you some questions first,' he told her. 'They want to try to catch these damned rebels, and any information you can give them will help.'

'But I don't know anything,' she protested. She knew that she did not want to help to catch the young men who had held her prisoner. They had treated her with comparative kindness. Even their threat to kill her had been a muted one.

'You saw them, didn't you? You saw their faces?'

She shrugged. 'Only in a very dim light. I wouldn't know any of them again. They were just ordinary young Indians.'

Stonor stared down at her, his brows drawn together in a frown. 'Marie, are you trying to protect them? Because if you are, let me remind you that the next person they kidnap may not be so lucky. They can't be allowed to get away with this, you know.'

'I'm not hiding anything!' she protested. 'I don't know anything which could help.'

Then Stonor walked to the door and opened it. There was a slight pause as he spoke to the sentry outside, then he came back to join her.

'Better sit down,' he said. 'This will take some time.'

'I'm so tired, Stonor,' she said unhappily. 'And I'm hungry. Can't it wait?'

The King came hurriedly into the room. He smiled at them both in a friendly fashion.

'All is well between you? Good. Now, Miss Brinton, I must ask you a few questions, then I will send you back to Mrs Cunningham by car so that you may relax in the peace of the bungalow. Or if you prefer, you may stay here in the palace near Mr Grey.' His eyes twinkled. 'Which would you prefer?'

'I think I'd better join Mrs Cunningham, sir,' she said.

'I understand that she's been very worried about me, and I wouldn't want her to go on being worried for much longer.'

'You are very thoughtful,' he said. He glanced at Stonor. 'Won't you sit down, Mr Grey?'

Stonor sat down beside Marie on the low couch. He leaned over and took her hand firmly.

She looked at the King with caution.

'First, Miss Brinton, can you tell me the names of any of these men?'

She shook her head.

'They did not once address each other by name in your presence? Are you quite certain of that?'

She nodded. 'Quite sure.'

The King looked depressed. 'They are cleverer than I had thought. Well, then, where were you held? Did you recognise anything about it?'

Marie explained that she had been held in a house at which she had arrived and from which she had left in darkness.

'The room was always shuttered. I have no idea where the house was.'

'Was it in a town? Could you hear any sounds which might give us a clue?'

'It was in the country, I think,' she said. 'I heard cows, and the wind rustling in trees.'

'You never heard any sound of vehicles? Any voices outside? Sounds from other houses?'

'Nothing like that. It was very quiet, I noticed that.'

'Was it marshland?' Stonor asked. 'You must have noticed what sort of country you drove through?'

'I was blindfolded,' she explained.

'What sort of roads were they? Main roads or cart tracks?'

'Rough hill roads,' she said.

Then Stonor pounced. 'Hill roads? How do you know they were hill roads?'

She looked at him crossly. 'We were coming down them at that sort of speed and angle. I could just tell we were driving down hills.'

'Good,' said the King. 'That is one solid point, anyway. A village in the hills, an isolated house.'

'It wasn't a village,' she said quickly. 'I'm sure I would have noticed sounds from other houses.'

'A farm,' Stonor said quietly. 'The cows indicate that, surely. A small hill farm.'

The King nodded. 'There are only a few hundred of them,' he said grimly. 'If it takes us a year we will search every one.'

'Did they talk to you?' Stonor demanded of her. 'Surely they spoke?'

'They only spoke when they had to,' she told him. 'In fact, I only saw one of them more than once. He had the gun.'

Stonor swore. 'Did he threaten you? Hurt you?' His eyes were wild with rage.

She shook her head. 'He never hurt me at all. He was really quite polite.'

'So he did speak to you?' Stonor had taken over the questioning, while the King sat silently watching them shrewdly.

Marie glared at Stonor. 'He spoke occasionally. It was he who dictated that letter to you.'

'But not the postscript?' he suggested softly.

She flushed, remembering all the words she had not written but had longed to put down. 'No, I wrote that.'

'Could he read English? Why didn't he cross it out? It was hardly a message to scare the hell out of me.'

'He very honourably allowed me to write a few words which he didn't read.' She hesitated, then said, 'He thought I was writing a love letter, you see. He thought it would make you more anxious to find me. And, don't you see, he was so sure I knew nothing that could help you that he didn't even ask to read it!'

Stonor glanced at the King.

The King sighed. 'That sounds obvious enough, does it not? Why else should he permit her to write a private message?'

Stonor shrugged. 'Then if that is all, your highness, may I accompany her to the bungalow?'

'No,' Marie said quickly. 'Jess will have enough on her plate without you descending on her, Stonor. I'll go alone.'

Stonor looked obstinate, but the King smiled at him. 'She will be safe. I will send six soldiers to guard her.'

So Marie drove back to the bungalow in a car driven by Aziz, who was looking somewhat subdued now. The soldiers rode behind them on horses, two abreast.

'What's wrong?' she asked Aziz.

'Everything,' he told her. 'In all this trouble, somehow my cousin the King has found out about Aissa and myself, and has ordered that I must not see her again under such circumstances. I think one of the servants was afraid that the King might order severe punishments when he found out that I have been seeing Aissa every day, so he hurried to betray us in order to avert the hand of calamity.'

'Was the King very angry?'

'Furious,' Aziz said grimly.

'What will he do now?'

'He has said that he will arrange a marriage for Aissa at once,' Aziz said sadly. 'I begged him to relent, but he was so angry I was forced to leave the room. He threatened to choke me to death!'

Marie suppressed a smile at Aziz's indignant tone. 'Poor Aissa ... I wonder what sort of husband he'll find for her?'

'God knows,' Aziz said miserably.

'I'm sure he'll try to find her someone near her own age,' Marie said comfortingly.

Aziz looked at her with wild eyes. 'Do you say that to torment me? Am I a stone that I can hear such news without bleeding inside?'

'I'm sorry,' she apologised, aghast. 'I ... I thought you would prefer her to have a chance of happiness instead of being forced into marriage with someone twice her own age...'

They drew up outside the bungalow. Aziz murmured goodnight, his head averted. She went slowly up the path and the door burst open.

'Marie! Oh, my dear girl...'

'Hallo, Jess,' she smiled.

Jess hugged her tightly, half in tears. 'How can you sound so calm? I've been frantic. Can you ever forgive me? This has all been my fault—I should never have brought you here in the first place. You must have been so scared.'

'Oh, it wasn't so bad!' Marie said casually.

'Are you having me on?' Jess stared at her incredulously.

She laughed. 'No, really. They were quite kind, honestly. I was a bit scared at first, but they never tried to frighten me.' She remembered the moment when they had said they would kill her and shivered suddenly. 'Well, they never threatened me directly.'

'My dear, they said they would kill you,' Jess protested, open-mouthed.

'Yes, they said that to me, too. I'm not sure if they meant it. I thought they did at the time, but now I'm not certain. They were none of them really the violent type.'

Jess gave a low groan of astonishment. 'I can't get over your calmness. You're very brave, Marie. I would have been gibbering inside twenty-four hours. I have a tendency to claustrophobia—that's why I spend so much time in the open. I hate to be shut up inside four walls.'

'Just as well they didn't kidnap you, then,' Marie smiled. 'They kept me locked in one room for the whole time.'

Jess put an arm around her. 'Come and tell me all about it while I watch you eat. You must be hungry.'

'I'm starving,' she admitted.

'Peter has given me a pile of tins of English food,' said Jess, her eyes triumphant. 'He was quite distracted with worry. He wanted you to have an English meal if ... when you got back.'

Marie looked at her affectionately. 'How kind of him. I can hardly wait!'

An hour later, full of cream of tomato soup, sliced cold ham, new potatoes and peas, and some tinned peaches to round off the meal, she sat contentedly watching Jess do a rough sketch of her.

'For Peter,' Jess told her with a smile. 'I gather from the palace grapevine that Peter is in for a big disappointment.'

Marie flushed. 'I'm afraid so. I liked him a lot, but...'

'But Stonor Grey is going to scoop the jackpot, as usual,' Jess nodded. 'So Rahaib was telling me. I was amazed, I didn't think you even liked the man.'

'I'm not sure I do,' Marie laughed sheepishly.

Jess looked concerned. 'My dear, are you sure you're doing the right thing? Stonor Grey isn't an easy man to deal with. He would make a rotten husband.'

Marie looked down at her hands, linked in her lap.

'The trouble is, Jess, I'm crazy about him,' she sighed.

Jess watched her shrewdly. 'I see. Like that, is it? And he?'

Marie felt her cheeks glowing. 'He ... feels the same way, he says.'

'Rahaib certainly said he was quite demented when you were missing,' Jess murmured. 'He was furious with Rahaib for letting it happen. He threatened to tear him limb from limb if you weren't found.'

Marie laughed. 'His bark is worse than his bite. How is Rahaib, by the way?'

'Fine. He had a bit of a bump on his head, but apart from a headache, he got over that quickly enough.' Jess grinned. 'I think it was his pride that suffered the worst blow. He was taken in by a simple trick like that. Poor Rahaib! He'll never forget it.'

'How could he have anticipated such a thing? He

shouldn't blame himself. Anyway, all's well that ends well.'

'Not for Jedhpur, it doesn't,' Jess said grimly. 'The National Park scheme will have to be shelved until they find another rich man to back it.'

'I expect Stonor will see that they do,' said Marie. 'He told me he wanted no more to do with it, but he knows other firms who would be interested. The King will get his tourist centre in the end.'

'You look tired,' Jess sighed. 'I shouldn't let you stay up talking. Off to bed now, my dear.'

'I would love a bath first,' Marie said. 'You can't imagine how much I longed for one in that stuffy little room. The smell of curry seemed to linger for hours.'

Jess made a face. 'How ghastly! By all means have a bath. Then sleep as long as you like. Lispa is so good with Jeremy that you won't be missed.'

Marie hesitated. 'Jess, I . . .'

Jess smiled at her. 'I think I know what you're going to say. Mr Grey wants to whisk you away from us?'

'I'm afraid so,' Marie admitted. 'He says he'll send someone else to take my place.'

'I don't think I need anyone,' Jess said calmly. 'Lispa will go on taking care of Jeremy for me. He plays with her boys and has a marvellous time. I can teach him to read and so on when the time comes. For the present I think I'll just let him grow up alongside Lispa's sons.'

'He'll turn into a little Hindu,' Marie laughed.

'He'll certainly learn more tolerance than he would have done back home,' Jess agreed. 'So don't worry. You can go back home with your man and marry him. You deserve to be happy.'

Marie kissed her, then went off to have a long, relaxing bath before tumbling into bed to sleep the clock around.

When she woke up she found Jeremy sitting on her bed staring at her unwinkingly.

'Hallo,' he said. 'I thought you were dead.'

'Well, I'm not,' she retorted.

'Did bandits kidnap you?'

'Sort of bandits,' she agreed.

'Were you scared?'

'Now and then.'

He considered her. 'I wouldn't be scared. I would hide and they would never find me.'

'Good idea,' she said solemnly.

He jumped off the bed. 'Mum said to tell you Mr Grey was coming in an hour, so do you want something to eat?'

Marie sat up. 'Yes, please. I'm hungry.'

Jeremy eyed her. 'So am I. I'll have another breakfast with you, if you like, to keep you company.'

She laughed. 'You'd better ask Mummy first.'

Jess looked at her with pleasure when she entered the living room. 'You look much better this morning. You looked a bit dead last night.'

'I was dead beat,' she nodded.

'What about breakfast? There's fruit and bread and a few eggs.'

'That will be lovely,' she said eagerly.

Jeremy begged to join her in her meal, but Jess drove him away. 'Little pig, he eats far too much in that kitchen. Stonor Grey will be here soon. Apparently he's determined to get you back to England today.'

'Today?' Marie stared at her incredulously.

Jess laughed. 'A man of lightning decisions, apparently.'

'He can't! I'm not even packed!'

'That can be dealt with in a flash,' Jess said easily. 'I'm not sure whether it's a good idea or not. You've had a bad shock, even though you've taken it so well, and I can't make up my mind whether or not it's wise to fly you back to England so quickly. You need some peace and quiet, in my opinion, but I may be wrong.'

Marie stared at the table. 'I think I would like to be back home.'

'Well, it's true that the monsoon weather will be starting soon, and that can be pretty devastating for anyone. Perhaps you should leave before the heat becomes unbearable.'

Lispa came in with the food, smiling warmly at Marie. While she ate her breakfast, Jess talked to her. 'Lispa can pack for you while you talk to your young man.'

'My young man!' Marie giggled. 'It hardly describes Stonor, does it?'

Jess laughed. 'No, not really. He's pretty impressive, isn't he? A bit like a monolith.'

Then Stonor was in the room, and Marie hardly noticed as Jess discreetly slipped away.

He kissed her hungrily, awaking her sleeping pulses. 'Darling, I'm so glad to see you,' she said, touching his face tenderly.

'Are you packed?' he demanded. 'I'm taking you home before all hell breaks loose.'

'What do you mean?' She stared at him in bewilderment.

'Aziz has run off with Aissa,' he said grimly. 'The

King is furious. He was swearing vengeance on his cousin when I saw him this morning. I think we should get out today. Life at the palace is going to be very hectic after this.'

Marie looked anxiously at him. 'What will the King do?'

'What can he do? Apparently they flew off in a private plane, nobody knows where, leaving a note which said they were getting married. Lord Hathni is even angrier than the King. He'll lose face because his son is breaking a betrothal.'

'Oh, dear,' Marie said faintly. 'I think you're right —we must go home at once. I think the air here is too stormy.'

Stonor lifted her out of her chair. 'Say goodbye to Jess and the little boy. I want to get you all to myself as soon as possible. I can't wait another week to marry you. We'll get a special licence when we get home.'

'Are you sweeping me off my feet, Stonor?' she teased.

'That's right,' he retorted. 'I'm going to make sure you don't escape me ever again. Consider yourself my prisoner for life.'

She slid her arms around his neck and lifted her face to his. 'You really are just a desert barbarian at heart, aren't you?'

The dark eyes burned down at her. He smiled adoringly and their lips met. Against her lips he whispered, 'There's a saying in my mother's country: what the desert claims, the desert keeps ... remember that, my darling.'

 **Harlequin**

# COLLECTION
## EDITIONS OF 1978

Harlequin's ✦ Collection 12

ANDREA BLAKE
**Night of the Hurrica**

Harlequin's ✦ Collection 106   1.25

ANNE WEALE
**If This Is Love**

**50 great stories
of special beauty
and significance**

**$1.25**
each novel

In 1976 we introduced the first 100 Harlequin Collections—a selection of titles chosen from our best sellers of the past 20 years. This series, a trip down memory lane, proved how great romantic fiction can be timeless and appealing from generation to generation. The theme of love and romance is eternal, and, when placed in the hands of talented, creative, authors whose true gift lies in their ability to write from the heart, the stories reach a special level of brilliance that the passage of time cannot dim. Like a treasured heirloom, an antique of superb craftsmanship, a beautiful gift from someone loved—these stories too, have a special significance that transcends the ordinary. **$1.25 each novel**

## Here are your 1978
# Harlequin Collection Editions...

Original Harlequin Romance numbers in brackets

# ORDER FORM
## Harlequin Reader Service

In U.S.A.
MPO Box 707
Niagara Falls, N.Y. 14302

In Canada
649 Ontario St.,
Stratford, Ontario, N5A 6W2

Please send me the following Harlequin Collection novels. I am enclosing my check or money order for $1.25 for each novel ordered, plus 25¢ to cover postage and handling.

| | | | |
|---|---|---|---|
| ☐ 102 | ☐ 115 | ☐ 128 | ☐ 140 |
| ☐ 103 | ☐ 116 | ☐ 129 | ☐ 141 |
| ☐ 104 | ☐ 117 | ☐ 130 | ☐ 142 |
| ☐ 105 | ☐ 118 | ☐ 131 | ☐ 143 |
| ☐ 106 | ☐ 119 | ☐ 132 | ☐ 144 |
| ☐ 107 | ☐ 120 | ☐ 133 | ☐ 145 |
| ☐ 108 | ☐ 121 | ☐ 134 | ☐ 146 |
| ☐ 109 | ☐ 122 | ☐ 135 | ☐ 147 |
| ☐ 110 | ☐ 123 | ☐ 136 | ☐ 148 |
| ☐ 111 | ☐ 124 | ☐ 137 | ☐ 149 |
| ☐ 112 | ☐ 125 | ☐ 138 | ☐ 150 |
| ☐ 113 | ☐ 126 | ☐ 139 | ☐ 151 |
| ☐ 114 | ☐ 127 | | |

Number of novels checked @
$1.25 each =                                          $ _____

N.Y. and N.J. residents add
appropriate sales tax                            $ _____

Postage and handling                          $ ___.25

                                        **TOTAL** $ _____

NAME _____

_____(Please Print)_____

ADDRESS _____

CITY _____

STATE/PROV. _____

ZIP/POSTAL CODE _____

ROM 2206

Offer expires December 31, 1978

And there's still *more* love in

# Harlequin Presents...

# Do you have a favorite Harlequin author? Then here is an opportunity you must not miss!